One Night in the Bayou

Miss Fortune World (A Miss Prim & Proper Mystery), Volume 2

Caroline Mickelson

Published by J&R Fan Fiction, 2018.

ONE NIGHT IN THE BAYOU

First edition. August 16, 2018.

Copyright © 2018 Caroline Mickelson.

ISBN: 979-8201217167

Written by Caroline Mickelson.

Chapter One

"SANGRIA SUNSET! THIS is my all-time favorite. Oh, and look at this one, I love this color too." I lifted a bottle of nail polish from the box on the counter in front of me and turned it upside down so I could read the name of the shade. "Parisian Pink. How perfect." I held the bottle next to my fingernails and nodded approvingly. The demure shade of pink was genteel, ladylike, refined. Essentially, it was everything I aspired to be. I smiled at Walter. "Thank you for placing this special order for me, Mr. LeBlanc."

"Call me Walter, please," the owner of Walter's General Store, who was also the uncle of Sinful, Louisiana's, Deputy Sheriff Carter LeBlanc, nodded his head. "I'm glad you're satisfied, young lady. Why don't you finish taking a look through your order and make sure everything you need for your camping trip is here."

"We're not going camping," I corrected him. "We're going glamping."

"Glamping?" Walter's brow knit in confusion. "I don't follow."

"Lucky you." My Aunt Ida Belle tossed a package of beef jerky onto the counter. "Give me plain old "sleeping in a tent, cooking over a fire" style camping over this new fangled glamour camping crap any day."

"Now, Aunt Ida Belle, you agreed that you were going to keep an open mind," I reminded her. I hadn't known my great-aunt for very long, less than two weeks actually, but it was obvious to anyone with a functioning set of eyeballs that she wasn't a woman who coveted luxury.

We might well be related by blood, but we were as different as night and day. Take the way we were dressed as the perfect example. Aunt Ida Belle had on a pair of well-worn denim jeans that were probably manufactured in the early nineties, a faded Coors beer t-shirt, and a pair of boots that would have looked far more appropriate on a construction site than on the feet of a woman her age. By contrast, I wore a white cotton blouse with cap sleeves, a multi-colored floral cotton skirt, and a pair of low-heeled lemon yellow sandals.

Aunt Ida Belle and her friends had not only welcomed me upon my arrival in Sinful, they'd managed to save my life when I'd been kidnapped by members of the Russian mob. This was no small thing, and I was more grateful than I could ever say.

"So you're Miss Prim and Proper, eh?" Walter asked.

I looked up and smiled. He seemed like such a pleasant man, by far the most normal person I'd met in this town. "That's right, I am. At least as long as my job at the newspaper holds out."

"You need to get back to Boston in a real hurry then?"

"Not just yet," I answered. "My editor said he'd run some of my old columns until I send him some new ones. He suggested I write a series on Southern manners."

"Well, here's your first tip," Walter said, his eyes darting over to where my aunt was looking at some fishing tackle. "Keeping your elders waiting isn't considered very polite in southern society." When he smiled, his eyes crinkled at the corners.

"Duly noted, Walter. Thank you." I turned my attention back to the box of supplies. The box held a new makeup kit, several bottles of nail polish, fluffy hand towels, facial masks, and a set of body lotions from my favorite Swiss spa. "It looks like everything is here. Oh, except for the champagne flutes I ordered."

"Champagne?" Aunt Ida Belle crossed over to the counter and looked between Walter and me with a disgusted expression on her face. "I don't know which one of you is more crazy. You, Stephanie, for thinking that Gertie, Fortune, and I are up for this level of nonsense, or you, Walter, for setting me up like this. You know I don't cotton with all this girly stuff."

I watched as an amused smile spread across Walter's lined face. Ah, so it was true. Gertie had filled me in on his unrequited feelings for my aunt, but I wasn't sure how fanciful she was being. Now I could quite clearly see a great tenderness in the way he looked at her. I didn't try to hide my smile.

Maybe this whole glamping adventure was going to be more productive than I thought. We could give Aunt Ida Belle a makeover and then invite Walter over for a candlelit dinner.

"I have your glasses packed up with the wines you ordered," Walter said. "I'll have Scooter deliver it along with your food order in about an hour. That okay?"

I opened my mouth to express my gratitude, but my aunt cut me off.

"No, it's not okay. This is about the most fool thing I've ever been talked into. Wine glasses on a camping trip?" She narrowed her eyes. "And what's this about food? What's wrong with taking some hot dogs and roasting them over a fire, huh?"

"Nothing is wrong with hot dogs," I hurried to assure her. The last thing I wanted to do was get this trip off on the wrong foot. "You've all been so warm and welcoming to me since I arrived here in Sinful that I wanted to do something special for you."

Walter's eyes twinkled. "I saw some smoked oysters in your box of goodies. You'll like that, won't you, Ida Belle?"

She groaned. "Just shoot me now."

And then, realizing how ironic her word choice was, her eyes met mine and an unspoken understanding passed between us. A shooting, namely mine, was exactly what we were trying to avoid. I'd been walking around Sinful with an invisible target on my back.

The Russian mob, specifically the Sidorov family, was after me. Based on a tip from an organized crime unit back in Boston, we had every reason to believe that this was the weekend that Boris Sidorov planned to avenge his son's death by taking my life. I reached up and touched my pearl necklace for comfort. As brave a face as I was attempting to put on, I was more than a little scared, so I welcomed the chance to distract myself with a girls-only glamping trip. Although I knew my companions were reluctant participants, I also knew they were willing body guards. And I was grateful. Deeply and desperately grateful.

"Well, let's work on *my* order now," Aunt Ida Belle said. "I want some corn chips and cheese dip to go with that jerky. Let's see, how about a twelve pack of beer and some ear plugs to drown out Gertie's snores." She looked around the store as if she was taking a silent inventory of what she'd need for our weekend away. "That ought to about do it, Walter." She opened up her wallet and drew out a small wad of bills, which she handed over to him.

He counted them out but she'd given him too much. He held out a couple of twenties, but she waved them away.

"Tell you what, Walter," she said, intentionally not meeting my gaze, "why don't you do me a favor and throw a couple of extra rounds of ammo in that box for me?"

AS GERTIE'S BEAT-UP, rusted-out old Cadillac bumped over a rutted road somewhere deep in the Louisiana Bayou, I made a mental note to add a chauffeured limousine to my list of glamping must haves for our next trip. During my short time in Sinful, I'd grown accustomed to what I called "Gertie's Wild Rides", but now she was giving *speed demon* a whole new meaning. As the Caddy hit a rut, I bounced up and hit my head against the roof of the car. Ouch. Glamping and concussions, not a good mix.

"No complaining allowed," Gertie called out in a pre-emptive effort to forestall our inevitable protests. "Focus on the bright side, at least no one's riding in the trunk. They'd have fallen out a mile back."

I looked over at Fortune, who sat beside me in the back seat. "What is she talking about?"

"You don't want to know." Her smile was rueful. "Seriously."

If I could tell you how many times I'd heard that since I'd arrived in town, you wouldn't believe me. It was as if Aunt Ida Belle, Gertie, and Fortune had a shared understanding of, well, just about everything that happened in Sinful. The dynamic between my aunt and Gertie, I understood. They'd been friends since before forever. Their relationship to Fortune was a little more difficult to decipher.

Fortune, aka Sandy Sue Morrow, was the niece of a close friend of theirs who had recently passed away. Fortune, who hadn't arrived much before I had, was spending the summer in Sinful cataloguing her aunt's estate. Which, I figured, she must do in the middle of the night, because I'd never seen her actually work on the massive project. But then, this discrepancy shouldn't surprise me. Fortune was nothing if not a contradiction in terms.

Fortune was blond with bright blue eyes, beautiful skin, and a trim, athletic figure, so it was easy to believe that she was the former beauty queen she claimed to be. But there was another side to her personality that made me wonder what I wasn't being told about her. She was watchful, wary, and reactive, none of which appeared to concern my aunt and Gertie. Quite the contrary, actually. While they weren't overly obvious about it, I sensed their desire to protect her.

From just what, I didn't know. And truthfully, it wasn't any of my business. If anything, I should take a page out of Fortune's book and sleep with one eye open too.

I was shaken from my reverie when Gertie slammed on the brakes and we all pitched forward and then backward in our seats. The seatbelt was no match for Gertie's driving.

"We're here," she called out. "All in one piece, I'll point out."

"No thanks to you," Aunt Ida Belle grumbled. "Your driving is so far beyond insane that there are no words to describe it."

Gertie turned in her seat, an "oh, yeah?" expression clear on her wrinkled face. "If that's true, then why am I the one who's always driving?"

"Because you're the one who needs the most practice," my aunt shot back.

Fortune caught my gaze and rolled her eyes. I shared the sentiment in spades.

I reached for the door handle. "Well, since we're here, let's start unloading our glamping goodies."

"Hold up," Fortune said. "Let me just take a quick peek around first." Without waiting for anyone to agree or argue, she slid out of the car and approached what was to be our home away from home for the next few days.

I craned my neck to watch as she approached the cabin. Although it was late afternoon, there was plenty of light left to see by. A quick glance around assured me that my instincts were correct. We were smack out in the middle of Nowhere, Louisiana. The cabin in front of us, halfway between semi-disrepair and somewhat maintained, was the only building of any sort in view.

"Have you been here before?" I asked.

Gertie and Ida Belle exchanged a quick look before my aunt answered me. "No."

I resisted the urge to ask more questions because I knew that when Aunt Ida Belle was acting this circumspect, no number of questions would elicit any further information. I'd have to wait and see. I turned my attention back to Fortune, who was now mounting the front porch steps. My eyes widened as I watched her pull a gun from her waistband. She looked in each of the cabin's front windows and then eased open the door, all the while standing with her back to the wall like I'd seen on TV cop shows. I leaned forward. "What's she doing?"

"Picking daisies," Gertie said. "What does it look like she's doing?"

I bit the inside of my cheek. It wasn't like her to snap. If fun-loving, easy-going, super-crazy Gertie was on edge, something must be up. I forced myself to remain quiet.

Just a few minutes later Fortune bounded down the cabin steps and over to the car. She leaned down and looked through the driver's side window. "All clear, let's unpack."

And so we did. As we carried bags, hampers, and boxes in, I marveled at how we'd managed to fit so much in the Cadillac. Once everything was inside, I managed not to pepper my companions with questions. Instead I took a good look around. To my relief, the cabin was clean. Simple but tidy. Quite obviously, someone had been in to clean before our arrival. Buoyed by this knowledge, I set about turning the cabin into a luxurious sanctuary.

I insisted that the others have a seat and a cold drink while I worked. A proper hostess would do no less. As I bustled about, I could feel their eyes on me, but that didn't deter me. I'd gone to great lengths to make my plans, and I enjoyed watching my decorative vision unfold.

"What's all the pink crap you've got over the windows?" Aunt Ida Belle demanded. "And why in the Lord Almighty's name are you putting it up? The cabin already has curtains."

So it did. Ugly ones. I surveyed my handiwork before answering. "I think the pink tulle adds a feminine touch."

"It's touched alright," Gertie said.

"Are you sure you wouldn't like some help?" Fortune asked.

I smiled my thanks but shook my head. I couldn't be sure, but my gut instinct told me that interior design wasn't her forte. "I'm almost done."

Not ten minutes later, I set the last crystal candlestick in place on the cabbage rose covered table cloth I'd brought with me. I poured myself a glass of white wine and joined the others.

"It looks real...nice."

"Thank you, Aunt Ida Belle." I ignored the skepticism in her voice and acted like she'd complimented me. In her own roundabout way, I'm sure she meant to. "Now, before we begin our pampering, I've just one question for you all." I made eye contact with each of them in turn before I asked what had been on my mind ever since we'd arrived. "Why are the three of you acting like we're sitting ducks on the first day of hunting season?"

Chapter Two

MUCH AS I EXPECTED, all three of my companions issued
denials that anything was wrong. They ranged from dismissive
(Aunt Ida Belle), to confused (Gertie), to evasive (classic Fortune).
I sat quietly through their refutations, and only once they'd grown
collectively silent did I try again. "How about the truth this time?"
I focused my attention on my aunt. "Why don't you start first, Aunt
Ida Belle?"

Her frown was so ferocious that I swear it was etching a new
wrinkle onto her face in real time. "I thought we were here to do
girly stuff? So let's crack out that nail polish and get to gussying
ourselves up." All of this was delivered without her meeting my gaze
head-on, which, knowing my aunt, made her evasion tantamount
to a full confession.

I was right. Something was going on.

"Fortune?" I shifted so I could better see her. "Why would my
aunt ask Walter to add a few rounds of ammunition to her order?"

Fortune shrugged. "Maybe there was a sale on it? How should
I know?"

I shook my head. Why did I bother? Very soon after I met her,
I realized the word *elusive* could well be spelled *F-o-r-t-u-n-e*. But
Gertie was generally an easier nut to crack, so I turned my attention
to her. "Gertie? How about you tell me why everyone's so on edge?"

Her eyes widened and half a dozen expressions flitted across her face as I watched her scramble for something to throw me off track.

"Okay, here's the truth," she began in what I sensed was the wind-up to a whopper of a lie. "We're all nervous about this mani-pedi thing. We don't have your experience dolling ourselves up. Right girls?" She paused expectantly, but neither Aunt Ida Belle or Fortune rushed in to save her from the verbal quicksand she was floundering around in. "We're simple country girls who don't have your big city ways."

I cocked my head to the side. "Really? Fortune too? Because I've heard from a few people that she was a beauty queen with an extensive list of pageant wins to her name before she became a librarian. It's hard to believe that she doesn't know her way around an eye shadow palette."

No one said another word in her own defense. I resisted the urge to keep talking, knowing that I'd learn more if I waited them out. But talk about an uncomfortable silence. It was about as awkward as being trapped in an elevator with strangers at a nudist colony.

Just as I'd expected, Gertie cracked first. "For cryin' out loud, Ida Belle, just tell her. Otherwise she's just going to sit and stare at us like we're in a lineup. I'm too old to waste this much time."

"Go ahead, Aunt Ida Belle," I prompted her. It didn't escape my notice that she shot a quick glance in Fortune's direction. Fortune's nod was almost imperceptible. Almost.

"Oh, all right. Here's the deal. Carter shared with us that he got a tip from an organized crime task force in Boston that Boris Sidorov is on the move. Heading south."

South. Toward me. I shivered.

"Now, Stephanie, I need you to stay calm," my aunt continued. "Carter merely suggested that if we were going to take a little vacation, this weekend was as good a time as any. Just in case."

I sat back while her words swirled around in my brain. This was a shock—yet it wasn't. We all knew that the Sidorovs were going to try to avenge Misha's death. Never mind the fact that I didn't kill him. It was Boris' oldest son Vladimir who'd done the dirty deed. He was in custody awaiting a murder trial. How safe he was from his father's wrath, I didn't know. Nor did I care. It was my neck I was interested in saving. I reached up and touched my beloved pearl necklace.

"Say something, child."

The worry in Aunt Ida Belle's voice did nothing to make me feel better. Neither did the grave look on Fortune's face. "I guess I'm not surprised."

Fortune nodded. "No, we knew Boris would want revenge. Maybe it's a good thing that he's making a move so we don't just have to sit and wait."

Which brought us right back to my earlier assertion that we were sitting ducks. I glanced toward the pink tulle covered windows. Daylight was gone and night had settled in. Somehow that did little to comfort me. I closed my eyes for just a moment in an effort to center myself. A fit of hysteria, however tempting, was not going to be of any help. It certainly wouldn't be well-received by my companions. These women were tough. Reliable. I didn't know how or why they'd become that way, but I didn't want to be the weak link in the chain.

I wasn't as tough as my Aunt Ida Belle. I wasn't as wily as Gertie, nor was I as gutsy as Fortune. But I refused to be a shivering, quivering mess either. I stood up. "Let's pick out colors for our manicures." I ignored their surprised looks as I gathered up the bottles of nail polish. I settled onto the ottoman and balanced the box on my lap. "Gertie, we'll start with you." I pulled out two options and looked at the stickers on the bottom of the bottles. "Which sounds better, Tahitian Passion or Venetian Violet?"

"Passion all the way, baby." She leaned forward and looked at the selection. "You got any camouflage orange or swamp water green in there for Ida Belle?"

I laughed. Bless Gertie for her unflagging good nature. I felt a rush of affection for the women I was sitting with. They weren't prim, and they weren't proper, but they had nerves of steel and hearts of gold. If they were going to put on a brave face and meet the threat head on, so was I.

"IT LOOKS LIKE A BIRD crapped on your face." With her face only inches from Ida Belle's, Gertie chortled. "I gotta get a picture of this. Fortune, hand me my phone."

Aunt Ida Belle's hand shot up and grabbed Gertie's wrist. "Do that, old woman, and I'll feed you to the gators."

I clapped my hands together as if I were trying to quiet down a room full of rowdy kindergarteners for story time. "Enough, please. Gertie, come sit over here so I can start your facial." I patted the chair I wanted her to sit in. "And no talking, Aunt Ida Belle, or your face will crack."

"Again. For the hundredth time," Gertie said, obviously unable to let that opening slip by.

"Fortune, please don't touch your gun again. At least not until your fingernails are dry." I swear, it was like these women had never been to a spa party. "Now, who would like a glass of wine?" I waited, but not even the crickets answered my question. "I have a nice chardonnay or a lovely pinot grigio." Still no takers. They were holding out. They knew it and I knew it. I sighed. "I do have cold beer as well."

Gertie's hand shot up. "Sold!"

Aunt Ida Belle made a sound that sounded like "me too".

"Fortune?"

She shook her head with a wry smile. "Later, thanks. I'm going to take the first watch tonight so it's better if I wait." She waved her hands impatiently, which, I didn't bother to tell her, wasn't going to help the polish dry any faster.

I poured two beers into the wine glasses I'd brought and gave one to Aunt Ida Belle and one to Gertie. "Take small sips so you don't disturb your face masks," I instructed them. "I should have thought to pack straws."

After Gertie had several sips, I took her glass and had her lie back in the chair. I applied a lemon meringue mask to her face with a paintbrush. It took twice as long as it should have because of her giggle fits. As soon as she was done I ordered her to sit still and keep quiet, no small job for Gertie. I heated a damp white towel in the microwave and then carried it over to my aunt. "Now, just keep this on your face for a few minutes and then you can rinse with cold water."

I pretended not to hear her outburst of swear words when the hot towel touched her face. I patted her on the shoulder. "It's all in the name of beauty, Aunt Ida Belle, all in the name of beauty."

With both of the older women in one stage or another of their facial, I settled in the chair across from Fortune. I reached for the bottles of nail polish and took my time going through them.

"Just how nervous are you?" Fortune asked, her eyes intent upon me.

I held up a bottle filled with iridescent green polish with a hint of silver sparkle. "This looks perfect for summer, doesn't it? It's called Mermaid Swish. I think I'll try it."

Fortune reached over and plucked it out of my hands. "Stephanie, answer my question. On a scale of one to ten, how freaked out are you?"

I thought a moment. "A twelve," I finally said. "And I'm really, truly sorry that I've dragged all of you into this. Again."

Aunt Ida Belle mumbled something unintelligible. Realizing that her words were coming out in a garbled mess, she sat up and rubbed her face vigorously with her hot towel. When she was done, she tossed it on the table. "That's enough of that talk, young lady. You're kin. One of us now, you hear? If you're facing a threat, you won't face it alone."

"Thank you, Aunt Ida Belle." I forced myself to smile, even though her words really only made me feel worse. "But how long are we supposed to hide out here?"

Fortune leaned forward and rested her elbows on her knees. "Carter seems to think that Boris is going to make his move this weekend. He's working with a taskforce from New Orleans to monitor your aunt's house. He's also got officers watching my house, and Gertie's too."

"But what if Boris finds us here?" I asked.

"Don't worry about that," Gertie assured me. "Only two people know we're here, Walter and Carter. Now, Walter's sweet on Ida Belle, always has been and always will be. His nephew has the hots for Fortune, so neither one is going to rat us out. We're safe."

Safe. Wouldn't I love to feel as confident about that as she sounded? But I didn't. Not by a long shot. "I have an idea."

"Let's hear it," Gertie said.

I took a deep breath and rushed ahead, knowing that what I was saying was flat out crazy. But desperate times called for desperate measures. "What if I offered myself up to Boris as bait?"

No sooner were the words out of my mouth than my aunt was on her feet. "No way. Forget about it."

I stood. "Well, not as bait exactly, Aunt Ida Belle, I meant more as a decoy. Just to lure Boris close enough that law enforcement can swoop in and scoop him up."

"No. Not while there's breath in my body," she said.

Knowing she wouldn't budge, I turned to Gertie. "What do you think?"

"I think you're about as green as newly-sprouted spring grass. Honey, the mob is many things, and dumb usually ain't one of them."

I only had one more potential ally. "Fortune?"

She opened her mouth to speak, but her response was interrupted by the sound of a single gunshot from right outside the cabin door.

Chapter Three

"GET DOWN," SOMEONE shouted. I think it was Fortune, but I couldn't be sure. Not only weren't my ears working properly, my mind wasn't either. I stood rooted to the spot.

"Stephanie, what's wrong with you?" There was no mistaking my Aunt Ida Belle's less than dulcet tones. She jerked roughly on my arm, and I collapsed in a heap next to her.

I blinked rapidly. "What just happened?"

Gertie shot me an incredulous look. "The Easter Bunny is trying out a new jelly bean delivery system. What do you think just happened?"

I squeezed my eyes shut and then reopened them, but my wish went un-granted. I wasn't in the midst of a very bad dream. "What are we going to do?"

"Avoid being shot, let's start with that." Aunt Ida Belle rested her hand on my shoulder as she rose to a crouching position . I knew that she didn't need assistance standing, she just wanted to keep me from getting up. She needn't have worried. I wasn't into playing target practice.

"Where's Fortune?" She looked around the cabin, her eyes finally resting on the open front door. "Curse it, where did she go?"

Gertie popped up, hands on her hips, a frown on her face. "Lord above, Ida Belle, that girl reminds me of you at that age." She extended a hand down to me. "Come on, Stephanie. I think it's safe to get up."

I stood, no thanks to my knocking knees. These women talked about gunfire as casually as most people talked about a spring rain shower. I didn't share their blasé attitude. I straightened my skirt and looked around the cabin.

Unlike the first time that the Sidorov family had taken potshots at us, this time there were no signs of shattered glass. The windows were all intact.

"Gertie, call Carter." My aunt headed for the front porch.

Gertie whipped her cell phone from her pocket and flipped it open. "Wait, what should I tell him?"

"Run your Easter Bunny theory by him," Aunt Ida Belle called over her shoulder as she slipped out in to the nighttime darkness.

I paced the length of the cabin as Gertie put in a call to the Sinful Sheriff's Department. These three women might look to the world like two harmless senior citizens and a blonde bombshell, but they spoke and acted like big city homicide detectives. Or perpetrators. Sometimes it was hard to tell.

"It was a single shot." Gertie held out her arm to block my way when I finally worked up enough nerve to head toward the front door. She met my eye and held up one finger, indicating she wanted me to wait for her. When I nodded my agreement, she turned her attention back to the person on the other end of the line. Carter, I assumed. "We were sitting inside painting our fingernails, having a proper little chat like Southern ladies are wont to do, when we heard gunfire." She made a few noncommittal noises in answer to questions I couldn't hear, but I could sense her growing impatience. "Are you coming here or not, Carter? I'm missing all the action while you're playing twenty questions with me."

I strained to hear what was going on outside the cabin, but I couldn't hear anything, which was both reassuring and eerie at the same time.

"Yeah, that means they're out there," Gertie conceded. "I think so, let me check." She held the phone against her chest. "Stephanie, go and see if the girls are okay. Tell 'em Carter's having six fits."

My heart hammered in my chest as I made my way to the doorway. I poked my head out. My eyes took several long seconds to adjust to the semi-darkness. I took a quick look around but didn't see anyone other than Fortune and Ida Belle. They had their backs toward me and their heads were bent together in quiet conversation.

"Aunt Ida Belle," I called out, "Gertie's on the phone with Carter and he wants to know if you're okay."

She paused before answering. "The two of us are fine."

I leaned back in the cabin and gave Gertie a thumbs up. "She says the two of them are fine."

Gertie repeated this into the phone and then listened for a quick moment more.

Startled, I moved aside as Fortune joined me in the doorway. Her face was drawn and her expression solemn.

"Gertie, tell Carter he needs to get the medical examiner out here." She blew out a long breath. "We found a body."

FORTUNE'S UNEXPECTED pronouncement galvanized Gertie into action, judging by the way she rattled off the information to Carter. With her phone still pressed to her ear, she shot past Fortune and hightailed it out of the cabin. The news had the opposite effect on me. I was unable to do anymore than squeak out a single word. "Body?"

Fortune nodded, a distracted look on her face. "Young Caucasian female, no older than twenty-five."

I winced. So young. "Did you see anyone else? Surely she wasn't out here hunting all alone?"

She watched me for a long moment before she spoke. "She wasn't shot, Stephanie."

"Heart attack, maybe?" I asked, hearing the false hope in my voice. I desperately wanted to hear that this wasn't murder. "Hypothermia?" Something, anything, natural. Please God. "Fortune, am I right?"

She shook her head. "She was strangled."

"But I heard a gunshot."

"That was intended to get us outside so we'd find her."

Her sympathetic expression made me feel like an absolute wimp. Which I was, I admit. This whole murder business was new to me. New, and decidedly unpleasant.

Fortune glanced over her shoulder toward the open cabin door. "Look, I really should be out there with Gertie and Ida Belle. Will you be okay alone in here?"

I nodded and forced myself to smile, although I'm sure it turned out more like a grimace. "I'll be fine."

Her relief was palpable. Apparently standing guard over a dead body out in the dark of the night was preferable to sitting inside a cozy cabin with a woman whom she feared might descend into a full-blown fit of hysteria.

"Wait, Fortune," I called as she headed for the door. "How do you know you're safe out there? What if whoever did it is still around?"

"I'll explain later," was all she said.

BUT THE EXPLANATION, when it came well over two hours later, made no sense. In fact, it only muddied what were already very murky waters. I looked around the group who had assembled in the cabin, wondering if everyone else except me understood the situation.

Carter and Deputy Breaux had arrived surprisingly quickly after Gertie's phone call alerting them to the trouble we were in, and they brought with them a man I'd never met before. Neither had my companions, judging by their curious and slightly suspicious reaction to his presence. I found my gaze returning to him more often than was strictly polite, but this stranger wasn't like any man I'd ever seen before.

First of all, he was big. Tall, easily several inches over six feet. And he was solid, built as thick as a two-hundred-year-old oak tree that had been in my grandparents' yard when I was growing up. I'd never been able to wrap my arms around that tree and I doubted I could wrap my arms around this man either.

His shoulder-length black hair was pulled back in a low ponytail. His eyes, which he kept trained on Carter, appeared to be a dark brown color. His skin was deeply bronzed. Stoic was the perfect word to describe his bearing.

"Stephanie," Carter's voice cut through my reverie. "I know this has all been a shock to you." He followed the direction of my gaze. "You don't have to be worried about my colleague. He's here for a reason."

I nodded quickly and looked away, grateful for the cover story even though the reason I'd been staring wasn't because I was worried.

"Well, why is he here? Who is he, Carter? And why did you let Deputy Breaux take the body to the morgue without us?" Aunt Ida Belle stood beside where I sat perched on the edge of the sofa. Her arms were crossed over her chest and her voice was in full no-nonsense mode. "You tell us now or we clam up."

Carter's face flushed. I didn't blame him for resenting my aunt's brisk tone. Where had she ever learned to issue orders like that?

"We'll get to that in due course, Ida Belle," he said, his voice impressively calm. "I'll remind you that I'm leading this investigation, so I'll ask the questions."

"Well, get on with it, then," Aunt Ida Belle snapped.

Her waspish tone was hardly one a well-bred lady would employ under normal circumstances. But then these weren't normal circumstances. We'd come out here to glamp and now we were sitting around discussing a murder.

I snuck what I hoped was another discreet peek at the stranger. A tattooed snake began at his wrist and ran up the length of his arm, disappearing under his black t-shirt sleeve and reappearing around the other side of his neck. I shivered. I'd never seen such extensive body art before.

I jumped when my aunt poked my shoulder. "What?"

"Stephanie, Carter asked you a question."

I felt my cheeks redden. "I'm sorry, Carter. Can you repeat it, please?"

"I need you to take a look at the body."

My eyes widened. "You want me to look at a dead body? Why?" I sank back on the couch, as if the retreat into soft upholstery could save me from such a hideously unpleasant task.

"I want to know if you can identify the victim."

"But that's ridiculous," I protested. "I hardly know anyone in Sinful."

I watched as Carter glanced at the man he'd brought with him. He nodded in response to whatever unspoken question Carter had just asked him.

Fortune, who had been unusually quiet up until this point, cleared her throat. "I think you need to tell her, Carter."

A rush of heat swooshed through my body as all eyes turned to me. Whatever this news was, I wanted—no, make that needed—to hear it. "Go ahead, Deputy."

His eyes met mine. "I'm aware that you're too new to Sinful to be able to ID one of our residents, but I have a reason to believe you might know this victim."

"What reason?" I asked.

He held out an evidence bag. "This note was pinned to the victim's shirt."

Hands shaking, I took it from him. It was easy to see through the plastic, especially because the handwriting on the note was so large. The writing was decidedly crude and the message was downright chilling.

Tell Stephanie she's next.

Chapter Four

NEXT. I clutched my pearls as that ominous word reverberated through my mind like a Chinese gong in a quiet temple. I stared at the note for a long moment before I looked up and met Deputy LeBlanc's eyes. The concern I saw there only reinforced my fear. "That's hardly what I'd call a veiled threat."

He nodded solemnly. "The Sidorovs are calling you out, Stephanie. You had to know it was coming."

I nodded. I had known that Vladimir Sidorov's arrest for the murder of his brother Misha was not going to sit well with their father. Had I known that Boris would attempt to exact revenge? Yes. But did I think he'd be so blatant about it? No. I'd assumed that he'd try to slip poison in food meant for me, or that he'd hire someone to try to run me over. I glanced around the cabin, taking in five very somber faces. "What do I do now?" I asked.

Gertie was the first to offer up a plan. "We go out, guns blazing, lighting up the night with gunfire, letting those Sidorov suckers know that they're not getting Stephanie. We'll take them down in firestorm of flying bullets—"

Ida Belle clapped her hands together, effectively cutting off Gertie's vigilante monologue. "Hush up, Gertie. We need someone with some brain power to chime in. Now just listen up." She turned her attention to Carter.

We all followed suit. My Aunt Ida Belle was not usually one to defer, certainly not to law enforcement. So if she was this willing to hear Carter out, that meant she was worried. Which officially freaked me out.

With all eyes upon him, Carter cleared his throat. "Right, so we need a game plan. But it's a bit more complicated than catching a local thug who's only a threat to Sinful residents. That would be a situation totally within my jurisdiction." He cast a glance at the man beside him. "But as we all know, the Sidorovs head up a powerful organized crime syndicate."

"Tell us something we don't know," Ida Belle snapped. "We need a plan."

Fortune reached out and laid a restraining hand on my aunt's arm. Her action appeared to have the effect she desired. Aunt Ida Belle lapsed into a sullen silence.

"Go ahead, Carter," Fortune said. "We're listening."

"We've got a plan, Ida Belle. It's just not one you're going to like."

"Will it end up with Boris either dead or permanently locked up?"

"That's the goal."

Aunt Ida Belle frowned. "Then why wouldn't I like it?"

Instead of answering, Carter looked to the man beside him. "Do you want to take it from here?" After receiving a brief nod in response, Carter addressed the group. "This is Agent Kase Mayeux."

"Agent?" I asked, because everyone else was silent. Maybe they all understood what I didn't. "You mean, like with the Fish and Game Department?"

"F.B.I.," the man said.

My eyebrows rose. I don't know which surprised me more, that Agent Mayeux was a federal agent with the Federal Bureau of Investigations or that his voice was off-the-charts sexy. I glanced at the other women to see if they'd had the same reaction, but if they did, they were keeping it well hidden.

He stood, clearly a man accustomed to taking control of a situation. "The F.B.I. shares Deputy LeBlanc's desire to eliminate the threat posed by Boris Sidorov. We're here to work in conjunction with the Sinful Sheriff's Department to make an arrest. Several arrests, actually."

His words lent credence to his professional background. He spoke as if he were debriefing a room full of law enforcement agents rather than ladies who were camping. Glamping. I found his deep voice so mesmerizing that it wasn't easy to focus on his words. But since he was speaking about something that was likely to help me stay alive, I struggled to pay attention.

"What exactly are we going to do?" Aunt Ida Belle demanded. "And yes, before you ask, I used the word *we* deliberately. I don't care if you do work for the Foolish Bureau of Idiots, you're not leaving us out of it."

I shot a quick glance at the agent to see what he made of my aunt's assessment of his employer, but if he had a reaction, it wasn't showing. His face was impassive.

"As it would happen, there is a role for each of you to play in our plans," Agent Mayeux told her. "Of course, you have the right to opt out of the arrangement."

"We're in," Gertie piped up, and in true Gertie fashion she had to elucidate. "All in. One hundred percent. We're so in, you'll never get us out. You'll think we're moles, we'll go so deep underground—"

"That's good to hear," Agent Mayeux cut her off. The man was a quick study of human nature if he'd figured out that Gertie was long-winded when it came to speeches. "Because I'm going to need to arrest one of you. Tonight. For murder."

His pronouncement was met with stunned silence. We all exchanged shocked glances.

"But we haven't killed anyone," I finally protested.

"Boris Sidorov doesn't know that," he countered. "We want him to think that we're focusing on one of you for the murder of that poor young girl we found tonight."

Tentatively, I raised my hand. "I'll do it. You can arrest me."

He shook his head. "No. Not you."

I frowned. "But I want to help. All of this is my fault."

"Oh, you can help all right. But we'll get to your role later. First, I need one of your friends to volunteer to be arrested. It'll mean a stint in lock-up, but we'll make it as short as we can. And naturally we'll completely wipe out any evidence you were ever arrested when the mission is complete."

"I'll do it," Gertie said. She got to her feet and held out her wrists. "Take me in, I won't resist."

I watched as the FBI agent shot a questioning glance in Carter's direction. Yes, I wanted to tell him, she's for real. But I remained silent. Carter could handle this one.

"Gertie," Carter said, "I think it's better if you stay on the outside." He held up his hand to forestall her protests. "I know I can trust you to create holy hell once we lock up one of the other ladies. No one will do a better job than you will at causing a huge fuss."

Gertie preened. "You've got that right."

So, if I was to play some as-yet-unmentioned role, and Gertie was to protest the arrest, that left either Fortune or Ida Belle to be arrested. So, naturally it should be Fortune.

"I'll do it," my aunt volunteered. "I'm the natural choice."

I waited a split second for Fortune to protest, but she stayed quiet. I didn't bother to hide my annoyance. "That's not right, Aunt Ida Belle. Let Fortune do it. Unless she doesn't want to be part of the solution?"

There, I'd thrown down the gauntlet. Which, judging by the look on Fortune's face, was the last thing she'd expected me to do. But right was right, and wrong was wrong. And in my book, it was wrong to allow an old woman to go to jail for a crime that none of us had committed.

But it wasn't Fortune who spoke next, it was my aunt.

"I may be old, Stephanie, but I'm not so old I can't make my own decisions." She cast a challenging glance around the room, daring someone to defy her. "I'm the one who's going to jail. So don't anyone even think about arguing with me."

Those last words were directed to me. I bit the inside of my cheek. Hard. Aunt Ida Belle wasn't going to listen to a single objection of mine, so I stayed silent. But Fortune was going to get a piece of my mind later. A serious piece.

"So that's settled," Carter said.

"Not exactly." I cast a look in Fortune's direction but she just looked down, which only served to irritate me further. "What about Fortune? What is she going to do?"

Carter and his colleague exchanged a quick glance.

"It's your call," Agent Mayeux said.

Carter looked none too pleased but he nodded. "We're going to put her under house arrest, ostensibly for interfering in police business. Fortune, we'll fit you with an ankle monitor."

Her frustrated groan mollified me somewhat.

"Look," Carter said, "it's not like anyone's going to question why you were arrested. You've developed a bit of a reputation since you arrived in Sinful."

She didn't argue that point, but she did give voice to another concern. "How can I help protect Stephanie if I can't leave the house? What if you need me for backup?"

Agent Mayeux coughed discreetly. "I think between the F.B.I. and the Sheriff's Department, we've got it covered."

I glanced at Fortune to gauge her reaction to their plan. But, to my surprise, she didn't say anything. Even more odd, Aunt Ida Belle stayed quiet too, even though I could tell she was steaming. I looked over at Gertie. She was staring up at the ceiling, moving her lips, as if she were counting to one hundred. What was going on? I shook my head. I swear, I will never understand these women.

"What about me?" I asked. "What's my role in all this?"

Agent Mayeux's eyes drilled into me with the intensity of two dark brown laser beams. "You, Miss St. James, are the bait we're going to use to reel Boris Sidorov in.'"

His suggestion was the same one I'd made earlier. I liked the way this man thought. I nodded. "I'll do it."

ONCE THE PLAN WAS AGREED upon, Carter made a quick phone call to Deputy Breaux telling him it was time to set things in motion. Within minutes, several squad cars with sirens blaring pulled up in front of the cabin. Aunt Ida Belle, already handcuffed, made her way down the cabin's front steps. The red and blue police lights were blinding in the otherwise dark night sky.

I stood helplessly by as Deputy Breaux read my aunt her Miranda rights. Despite the fact that Carter had warned us that they were going to make this whole charade look real, tears pricked the back of my eyes. There she was, my aunt Ida Belle, in handcuffs, being helped into the back of a police car. Because of me. This was so wrong. "Carter, no, you're making a mistake," I called after him as I came down the steps. "Please don't do this."

A young deputy held out his arm to stop me from getting any closer. "You'll have to stand back, miss."

Gertie came out of the cabin to stand beside me. Tears were streaming down her face as she slipped an arm around my shoulders. We watched as Fortune came down the stairs next. She also had restraints on her wrists. Her head was bowed and her hair hung over her face so her expression was hidden, but certainly any onlooker would see what we saw before us—a young woman carrying a heavy burden of guilt and shame on her shoulders.

I just couldn't go through with this. I didn't care if everyone else thought it was a good idea. It was asking too much of everyone. "Wait, Aunt Ida Belle, I've changed my mind—"

No sooner were those words out of my mouth than her head whipped around and she glared at me with a ferociousness that left me in no doubt about what she wanted me to do: carry on, see this through, and, for the love of whiskey, don't whine...I saw it all there in that one look.

"Call an attorney, Stephanie," was all she actually said before Carter shut the cruiser's door.

Helpless and hopeless, I watched as the sheriff's vehicles pulled away.

"Let's go, ladies." Agent Mayeux motioned to the cabin with a curt nod of his head. "Get in there, pack up your things, and I'll follow you back into Sinful."

Somewhat annoyed by his authoritative tone, I followed Gertie into the cabin. The lights were bright and my eyes took several minutes to adjust. Once everything was in focus, I turned my attention to Gertie.

"I'm so sorry that was hard for you, Gertie. You should never have had to—" but I broke off when I realized that not only were her tears now dried, her eyes were twinkling.

Gertie slapped her knees with her hands and almost fell over, she was laughing so hard. I stood and stared. Laughing? I glanced over at Agent Mayeux.

"Do you think she's in shock?" I asked him.

He merely shook his head.

"Lord above, don't that beat all," Gertie chortled. She drew herself up to a standing position and wiped away fresh tears of laughter. "Stodgy, bossy, fussy old Ida Belle hauled off by the cops. I love it! Never thought I'd see the day. Definitely a Sinful Ladies first!"

"But it wasn't real," I protested. Her reaction had to be shock. There was nothing else to explain it. "It was a part of our plan."

Gertie waved a dismissive hand. "Doesn't matter, it was still priceless. What I wouldn't give to have caught it on film. Hey, you know, I was watching one of those shopping at home network shows where the pretty young hosts just gab away, and I saw they were selling sunglasses that have a hidden camcorder in them. I'm gonna get me a pair. They'd come in real handy on a night like tonight."

I knew it was rude, but I just stood there and stared at her. Was she coming unhinged before my eyes?

"Ladies," Agent Mayeux's voice made it clear he had about two-tenths of an ounce of patience with us left, "gather up your belongings and lock up. I'll wait outside and I'll follow you back to Sheriff's station. Gertie, you need to be there to start kicking up a fuss. Miss St. James, you and I need to head to the morgue." Without waiting for a response, he headed out the door, shutting it rather loudly behind him. Clearly the F.B.I. didn't include a manners component in its agent training program.

Gertie and I didn't speak as we packed up everything we'd unpacked a few hours ago. As I folded the pink tulle, I felt a wave of regret that our lovely glamping weekend was ruined. I felt one thousand times worse that I'd brought so much trouble with me when I'd left Boston and headed to Sinful.

When we were finished cleaning up, Gertie and I stood and surveyed the cabin. I knew we needed to go, but I had a lingering question that I just had to ask. "Gertie, when Carter was explaining that one of us had to pretend to be arrested, why didn't Fortune volunteer?" It bothered me greatly that she was so willing to let my aunt sit in a jail cell. "I can't understand why she didn't offer."

Gertie laid a gentle hand on my shoulder. "She couldn't, Stephanie. She just couldn't."

"But why?"

Gertie studied me for a long moment, her expression suddenly sober. "Honey, because you're family, I'll tell you. But you have to swear on Elvis' grave that you won't tell a soul. Ever."

I nodded and crossed my heart. Elvis' grave. This had to be serious. "I swear."

"Fortune is an undercover C.I.A. agent who has an arms dealer named Ahmad trying to hunt her down and kill her. There's a price on her head, and she's here in Sinful to hide out."

Indignant, I grabbed my two bags of glamping supplies and, without a word, headed out of the cabin and into the darkness. Fortune a C.I.A. agent? Really?

Just how stupid did Gertie think I was?

Chapter Five

WE DIDN'T SPEAK FOR much of the ride back to Sinful. Frankly, I was still perturbed that Gertie had insulted my intelligence with her "Fortune is a CIA agent" story. Even if I had known how to address such an absurd fabrication, it would have been impossible to speak as we bumped over dirt roads. I had to keep my teeth clenched together so that I didn't bite off my own tongue. The silence didn't seem to bother Gertie in the least though. As if she didn't have a care in the world, she hummed show tunes, quite poorly I must add, as she raced back toward Sinful.

True to his word, Agent Mayeux followed us in his pick-up truck. I stared out into the darkened night, my mind filled with twelve dozen jumbled thoughts. Many of them were about the mysterious Agent Mayeux himself. He wasn't like any man I'd ever seen before, and a part of me was more than a bit frightened by his cold, detached demeanor. But another part of me, I had to admit, was intrigued by the way he carried himself. He was just one more character in a very colorful cast that populated my aunt's home town. "Sinful is such a strange place," I said aloud as we finally reached a paved road.

"Preach it, sister," Gertie chortled. "It sure isn't like Boston, I bet."

"It's not," I admitted. "Do you think Aunt Ida Belle is going to be okay tonight?" I cast a sideways glance at her, although it was too dark to see her properly. Still, I found her company strangely comforting. "Jail has to be frightening, even if it is a ruse."

Gertie reached over and patted my arm. "Listen, kid, I know you haven't known her long, but your Aunt Ida Belle is made of tough stuff. She's got a cast iron will and can survive anything. I bet you're not that different under all that fancy fluff."

Funny, but the way that Gertie referred to 'fancy fluff' sounded more like an endearment than an insult. "I don't think I am, Gertie. I'm scared."

She nodded, suddenly sounding uncharacteristically sage. "I understand that, but you've got a part to play. Focus on that. If we want this to be over with then we need to convince the Sidorovs that Ida Belle is really and truly under suspicion for murder. Our best chance of nailing them is throwing them off their game."

"Our best chance?" I frowned. "Surely you mean the FBI's best chance?"

She hesitated only a nanosecond. "Oh, right. Yeah, sure."

She peeled around a corner at close to fifty miles an hour. The glow of street lamps in the near distance reassured me. If Sinful was in sight then there was a decent chance that we might make it back in one piece. With Gertie's driving, you never really knew.

"So, you think you can play act your part okay, Stephanie?" she asked. "If it's easier, why not try for shell-shocked instead of righteous indignation? I bet people would buy that from you."

"I can do it," I said, hoping that I sounded more confident than I actually felt. "I mean, I have to, don't I? Aunt Ida Belle is counting on me."

"Atta girl." Gertie slammed on her brakes so hard that I was thrown forward and had to reach out and brace myself against the dashboard to keep from going through the windshield. I looked around in surprise. We'd reached the Sheriff's Department already. "Just remember," Gertie said, "that you can handle anything."

"I CAN'T HANDLE THIS. I just can't." I dropped my hand from the cold stainless steel door handle in front of me. I would have taken a step backward but Agent Mayeux was right behind me. So close, in fact, I'm sure I could have him arrested for trespassing on my personal space. I craned my neck and looked up over my shoulder at his impassive face. "I've never seen a dead body before."

"That's not strictly true, is it, Miss St. James?" His deep voice rumbled in his throat even though he kept his voice low. "What about the time you saw your boyfriend's body on the floor of Ms. Morrow's kitchen floor? Surely that counts."

"Misha wasn't my boyfriend," I protested for what had to be the hundredth time since my arrival in Sinful. "And no, I don't think it counts. I knew Misha. What I meant to say was, I've never seen a stranger's dead body before."

He reached around me for the door handle and pushed it open. "Well, there's a first time for everything." And with that bit of wisdom, he put a hand on my back and guided me into the morgue.

The cold was the first thing that hit me. And then the drab registered. I hardly expected a disco ball to drop from the ceiling, but everything was so gray, so colorless. There was a horrid sense of lifelessness about the place. I shivered.

"Let's get this over with," Agent Mayeux said.

My thoughts exactly.

We were greeted by a tall, lanky attendant with long dark hair that hung over his face like a mourning veil. His enthusiastic greeting was in stark contrast to our surroundings. "Welcome. Who are you here to see?"

My eyes went to the name badge pinned on his gray scrub top. Chris. "Hello, Chris." No matter my state of agitation, good manners were good manners.

"We're here to see the young woman just brought in," my companion said.

Chris rubbed his hands together with a bit more glee than I thought appropriate. I wasn't sure of proper morgue etiquette, but I don't imagine it was vastly different from funeral home etiquette. I glanced at Agent Mayeux, who now stood beside me, but his face was unreadable.

"She's something else, that one," Chris said. "Very interesting. I'm particularly intrigued by the bruising patterns around the neck. You see, with most cases like this there's more of a—"

Agent Mayeux held up his hand to forestall the lesson in strangulation that I most certainly didn't want to hear.

"Take us to the body."

Without another word, Chris nodded and motioned for us to follow him to a gurney where a body lay under a gray sheet. I couldn't remember ever wanting to do anything less than I wanted to view this body, but something, make that everything, about Agent Mayeux's body language told me I wasn't going anywhere until I'd had a good, long look. Why, I still couldn't say with any certainty. The chances of my knowing this person were one in a million.

Chris took hold of the sheet. "Ready?"

I nodded, unable to think of a way to verbally express my utter stomach-clenching dread at what was about to happen.

"We're not unveiling a royal portrait here," Agent Mayeux grumbled. "Pull back the sheet."

Chris did as bid.

At first my eyes wouldn't focus properly. All I saw were body parts. Hands laid to the side of the body in a very still, very unnatural manner. A chest that didn't rise and fall with the breath of life. Auburn red hair that framed an unexpressive face. A face I knew. Well.

I sucked in my breath as the room began to spin. "Cat."

"What?" Agent Mayeux put his hands on the sides of my arms and turned me around to face him. "What did you say?"

"Cat." I could barely squeeze out the single word. Tears welled in my eyes. This wasn't a nameless victim. This was someone I'd known for years. And now she was dead at the hands of the Sidorovs. Literally. Her neck was a horrible collage of ugly, discolored bruise marks. I closed my eyes against the vision of what the last seconds of her life must have been like.

Agent Mayeux shook my shoulders. "Miss St. James, I need you to cooperate with me here. Come on, snap out of it."

I opened my eyes but couldn't make myself look anywhere but into the federal agent's eyes.

"You recognize her, don't you?" he demanded.

I nodded. "Yes, I know her." Knew her. Bile rose in my throat. "I can't look again." I stared up at him. "Can we go? Please?"

"You don't need another look?" Chris asked.

"No." I shook my head vehemently. The vision of what I'd seen would never leave my mind. Not if I lived to be one hundred years old. Three times over.

"You can give me a rock solid identification?" Agent Mayeux stared down at me for a long moment and I found myself unable to look away. "Promise me before we go."

I nodded again but knew that wasn't what he wanted. He wanted words. "I can," I forced myself to say. "I promise."

He motioned for Chris to cover the corpse. I watched, relieved that I didn't have to look at the body any longer, but something about watching the sheet pulled over her face made the room spin around me. I probably would have hit the floor if Agent Mayeux hadn't reached out to steady me.

"Easy now, Miss St. James. The worst is behind you."

I stared up at him as the spots in front of my eyes faded away. Me? It wasn't myself I was sick about it. It was the still form of the woman I'd once known that lay unmoving on a cold steel gurney that sickened me. No life should end like this. And then, as if a bucket of freezing cold water had been thrown in my face, I gasped. "Priscilla."

Without a word, Agent Mayeux propelled me out of the morgue. His grip on my arm was firm, but under the circumstances I welcomed the support. A vortex of questions and frightening images swirled around my mind. Walking twenty-five feet without support seemed a herculean task.

Once in the hallway, he deposited me onto a hard wooden bench. "Who's Priscilla?" he demanded.

I had to tilt my head way back to be able to look at him. "Please sit down," I said, my voice weak to my own ears. "I hardly think it's polite to stand there towering over me as if I'm a common criminal."

He folded his arms across the chest. "I'm not in the business of being polite."

I leaned my head back against the wall. "This is so surreal that I don't even know what's going on or what I'm supposed to do."

"Well, I do. My job is to catch the bastards that killed Priscilla."

"Priscilla?" I covered my heart with my hands, as if the simple action could protect it. "Do you think something has happened to her?"

"I believe we just saw proof of that." His frown was like a tornado funnel heading toward a prairie town. It didn't inspire confidence that all would end well. "Wait, I thought you just assured me that you could positively ID the victim."

"Of course I can."

He took out his phone and looked at me expectantly. "Spell her last name for me."

It was my turn to frown. "Whose last name?"

He arched an eyebrow. "Priscilla's last name."

I touched my fingertips to my temples. A headache the size of Texas had settled in between my ears. "She doesn't have a last name."

His eyes narrowed. "Miss St. James, I'm asking you for the last time. What is the name of the murder victim?"

"Cat." Hadn't I told him this twice already?

"Cat?" His confusion mirrored my own. "Then who is Priscilla?"

"My cat."

"Your cat? Then who is that woman in there?"

"Please, Agent Mayeux, try to keep up. I've just had a horrible experience, I'm heartsick about what the Sidorovs have done, and I'm desperate to go and see how my Aunt Ida Belle is faring."

He plopped down on the bench across from me. When he spoke, his voice was dangerously low. "Miss St. James, may I remind you that I am a federal agent of the United States government?

That gives me the power to arrest any citizen who is obstructing justice. Do you understand me?"

I bit my tongue to leave unsaid some of the impolite comments that sprung to my mind. My exhaustion, my fears, and my ties to the Russian mob were not this man's fault, even if they had ended up being his problem. "Yes, of course I understand you, Agent Mayeux. But perhaps we could talk about your job another time? I think it's best if we get back to the subject at hand." I paused to give him a chance to speak but he didn't, so I forged ahead. "The woman we just saw is - was - Cat."

"Not Priscilla?"

"No, Priscilla's my cat. I believe I just told you that."

"You're testing my patience, Miss St. James." If his terse tone of voice was any indication, he was speaking the truth. "Forget about your cat. Tell me about Cat. The human Cat."

Forget about Priscilla? He might as well tell me to forget about breathing. But the one thing I did know was that if I didn't figure out what had happened to Cat, I wouldn't likely ever learn what had happened to Priscilla. I drew in a deep breath, exhaled, and squared my shoulders. "Cat is my cat sitter. Her proper name is—was—Catriona Carmichael."

He tapped this into his phone as I spelled her name for him. "Age?"

"I believe she's somewhere in her late twenties. I'm not certain because I hardly thought it polite to ask." Did that really need saying? Ladies did not press each other on such a delicate subject. Next he was likely to ask me her weight.

"Who's her next of kin?" he demanded, not looking up.

I thought a moment. "I only really know about Curtis. He's her everything, pretty much all she talks about." Tears filled my eyes. Poor Curtis. Whatever was he going to do now?

"Is Curtis her husband or her son?"

"Neither. Curtis is her cat."

His eyebrows rose. "Her cat?"

His incredulous tone set off a ripple of annoyance within me. "Yes, Agent Mayeux, Curtis is—was—her cat. Her prized Persian, just like Priscilla is mine. They're both beautiful animals, but I've always been partial to green eyed Persians, which my Priscilla is, whereas Curtis has—"

He held up his hand. "Stop right now. You're babbling. No one cares about the cats."

I stiffened. There he was wrong. I cared very much. But I held my tongue. I owed it to Cat to help the FBI avenge her death in whatever way I could, even if it meant I had to endure this man's company. "I don't know what else to tell you that will help. I've known Cat for several years in a professional capacity, but I don't know anything about her personal life."

He sat silently watching me for a long moment before he spoke. "Why is she here in Sinful?"

"I don't have a clue," I said, but we both knew that wasn't true. I did know the connection between the Sidorovs and Catriona Carmichael.

Me.

Chapter Six

DURING THE NEARLY HOUR-long ride from the hospital morgue to the Sheriff's Department, Agent Mayeux fired questions at me, one after another, as if he were at the shooting range and I were the paper target. I felt full of holes by the time we were less than a mile from the hospital. "I can't think what else to tell you," I protested.

"When's the last time you heard from Catriona Carmichael?" he asked.

I didn't bother to turn and look at him. It was still the dead of night and therefore dark. But I already knew that he'd be wearing an impassive expression that would give me no clue to what he was thinking. "I believe I've already answered that question, Agent."

"Well, answer it again."

I sighed. "The day before I left Boston, Cat came to my apartment to pick up Priscilla."

"Why didn't you drop your cat off at the kennel?"

Kennel? Really? Obviously this man knew nothing about the care and feeding of prized Persian cats. Under normal circumstances, talking about Priscilla brought me great joy. But now, not knowing where she was or what had happened to her, I couldn't bring myself to speak her name. "Cat doesn't run a kennel," I forced myself to answer. "She provides tender loving care in her home to select animals. A part of the service she runs..." but I was too choked up to continue.

"Take a deep breath," he told me. "You've had a shock."

I closed my eyes against the image of Cat's bruised neck. But doing so didn't erase what my mind's eye saw. "I'm okay."

"How did she seem when she came to your apartment? Did she act differently toward you in any way?"

I considered his question. It hadn't been that long since Cat and I had seen each other, a couple of weeks at most. But so much had happened since then that a part of me felt as if I'd been here in Sinful forever. I replayed her visit in my mind but there was nothing the least bit unusual about it. "I'm sorry, but I can't think of anything at all that would be helpful."

"When's the last time you spoke to her?" He exited the highway and turned left onto Sinful's main street. "Surely you've checked in on your cat recently?"

I winced. I was grateful that the truck was dark enough to hide my reddened cheeks as the realization hit me full on. I was the world's worst pet owner. The world's worst pet-sitting client. Adding the world's worst great-niece to the list wouldn't be inaccurate. Priscilla was heaven only knew where, Cat was dead, and Aunt Ida Belle was in jail. All because of me.

"I know it's overwhelming but just take it one question at a time." Agent Mayeux slowed his truck as we approached the sheriff's office. "I need you to focus."

"I am focusing." Focusing on what horror I'd inadvertently brought to innocent bystanders by my association with the Sidorov family. "But it's not a pretty picture."

We remained silent as he parked under a street light just outside the jail. I struggled to keep my tears from spilling while I waited for what I knew was coming. A reprimand issued courtesy of the United States government, one I richly deserved.

"A woman you knew is in the morgue," he started out with, his voice so low I had to lean in closer to actually hear him.

I nodded. I couldn't speak for the lump in my throat.

"Your aunt is in jail, subjecting herself to humiliation from the residents of Sinful until this is cleared up." He paused for a long moment. "And your cat is missing-in-action. Quite possibly the victim of a mob hit."

"I am painfully aware of this, Agent Mayeux."

He switched off the truck's engine and unfastened his seat belt. But when he reached for the door handle, I had to stop him. I needed to know what was going to happen next.

"Wait, just wait a second. Please." I took a deep breath. "What are we going to do?"

He nodded in the direction of the jailhouse. "I need to confer with LeBlanc."

I waved my hand to dismiss the obvious. "No, I meant, what is the plan to avenge Cat's death?"

Agent Mayeux slipped out of the truck and came around to open my door, the first display of proper manners I'd seen from him yet.

"Out you go." He issued the command as if I were a Labrador. So much for propriety.

With as much dignity as I could muster, I climbed down from the truck's cab. I looked up at him. "What are we going to do after we're done here?"

His lip curled up in a snarl. "You and I are going to team up and wipe that Sidorov scum off the face of this earth."

I nodded. That was a plan I could live with.

NO SOONER HAD WE STEPPED into the building than I heard Gertie raising heck.

"Just open the damn door, Carter," Gertie demanded in a voice loud enough to wake the entire town. "If you don't, I'm going to call the mayor."

"Aww, come on, Gertie," we heard Carter respond. "It's the middle of the night. And you know that the only thing scarier than Celia during the day is Celia at night."

"Who cares? She can get her beauty sleep another night. It's not like it's going help her anyway. That woman is so ugly—" Gertie stopped speaking when she saw us. Her eyes lit up as she pointed toward Agent Mayeux. "Ah ha, the cavalry has arrived. Finally. Where in the blue blazes have you two been?"

I glanced up at Agent Mayeux to see how he would respond to Gertie in action. But if I'd expected an outward display of surprise or any other emotion, I was mistaken.

I hurried to Gertie's side. "How's Aunt Ida Belle?"

"How would I know? Celia's pet deputy won't let me in to see her." She winked at me.

Good heavens, she was enjoying this. I stared at her in wonder. In even the most awkward and uncomfortable of situations, she managed to find fun. I didn't know whether to be horrified or inspired by her reaction to life. What I did know was that I craved a moment alone with my Aunt Ida Belle. She may lack Gertie's joie de vivre but there was something steady about her that I really wanted to lean on about now.

"Where's LeBlanc?" Agent Mayeux stood behind me. His voice rang with impatience.

Gertie threw her hands up in the air. "Hiding, I wouldn't doubt."

The door to Carter's office opened and he stepped out into the hallway. "I heard that." He greeted us with a nod as he stepped around us. "Let me just lock the front door so we're alone."

We waited in silence for him to return. I wouldn't have blamed him if he'd decided to lock the door with himself on the outside. Locking up my Aunt Ida Belle couldn't have been easy, and listening to Gertie wail had to be sheer misery. Poor Carter.

No. Poor Cat. She was what I needed to focus my attention on. The rest of us were working a plan. She deserved vengeance. I'm not going to pretend that I was over the horror of seeing her body in the morgue. Her death was a tragedy that would haunt me for the rest of my life, this I didn't doubt. But now that the first wave of tears had passed, something hardened in my heart. I was angry. Vigilante angry.

Carter came back around the corner, a grim look on his face. "I don't know how much time we have before words starts to get out that Ida Belle was arrested. It's going to be a zoo out there in short order."

Gertie nodded her agreement, but his words made no sense to me.

"But it's the middle of the night," I protested. "It will be hours before the sun is up, and surely it will take a few hours more, if not a few days, for word to get around."

Gertie, Carter, and Agent Mayeux exchanged amused glances.

"She's from Boston," Gertie said to the men by way of explaining my apparent ignorance. "Honey," she reached over and patted my shoulder, "in a town the size of Sinful gossip spreads like a wildfire. I'd bet the contents of my purse that the phone lines have already started buzzing."

"Which may not be an entirely bad thing," Carter chimed in. "We want word circulating that Ida Belle's been arrested for murder. The sooner Sidorov hears about it, the better."

I could feel frown lines form on my forehead as I tried to process that thought. "How do you think Boris is going to react when he sees that blame has fallen elsewhere?"

"He won't care." Agent Mayeux crossed his arms over his chest. "He doesn't want a connection to this. He just wants you to get the message that you're next."

I shivered. This was beyond surreal. I turned to Carter. "I'm ready to see my aunt now."

"I'm sorry, but I can't let you do that, Stephanie."

"Why ever not?" I cried. I whirled around to face the FBI agent. "Say something, do something, anything. Can't you pull rank?"

Instead of answering me, he gave Gertie a pointed look. "Why don't you two ladies have a quiet word while LeBlanc and I talk."

I opened my mouth to lodge a very vehement protest but stopped myself when Gertie laid a gentle hand on my arm.

"Let's do as they say," she said, steering me toward the other end of the hallway. She sat in one of two chairs set up against the wall and motioned for me to sit in the other.

A compliant Gertie? Could the night get any stranger?

"Stephanie, you need to stop fretting about Ida Belle. She'll be just fine."

I pointed toward the thick steel door that stood between us and lock-up. "She's in a jail cell, for crying out loud."

"She's been in worse situations, trust me. But we don't have time for those stories now. Maybe later."

Oh, no. Not maybe. Definitely later. These were stories I wanted to hear. Just so long as they weren't tall tales such as her "Fortune is a secret agent" lie.

"Now, did you see the body?" Gertie asked.

I blinked in surprise. I'd forgotten that she wasn't up to speed. No doubt Agent Mayeux was filling Carter in, so I did the same with Gertie. Her eyes widened when she heard that I'd recognized the corpse.

Gertie shook her head. "That poor girl. This just wasn't right."

That was the most rational thing I'd ever heard Gertie say. And the truest. It wasn't right.

"I just don't know what to do next."

Gertie nodded her head in Agent Mayeux's direction. "What does 'The Rock' have to say about your next move?"

I followed the direction of her gaze. She wasn't that far off the mark. Kase Mayeux's body was rock solid, not to mention that he was stone faced. "Precious little, actually. He hasn't told me where we're going next."

Gertie thought a moment. "Have you called Cat?"

"She's in the morgue," I said, surprise causing me to respond a little too loudly. The men at the other end of the hallway stopped speaking and turned to look at us. I made sure to lower my voice as I turned back to Gertie. "She's dead."

"I know that. Just because I'm old and wrinkled doesn't mean I'm a fool." Her gentle tone took some of the sting out of her words. "I meant, did you call her cell phone to see who answered it?"

I shook my head. "I hadn't thought of that."

She elbowed me. "Well, get going then before some yahoo from the Federal Bureau of Imbeciles gets their hands on it."

I reached into my handbag and took out my cell phone. My hands shook as I tried to dial Cat's number. After my fourth unsuccessful attempt, Gertie held out her hand and I gratefully handed the phone to her. From memory I rattled off Cat's cell phone number.

Gertie flashed me a thumbs up when someone answered. But then her forehead creased. "Take out or delivery? Lord above, an egg roll sounds heavenly just about now. But maybe some other time." She disconnected the call and raised an eyebrow. "Jade Palace?"

Oops. "Sorry, in times of stress that's the first number that comes to mind."

Gertie chortled. "I hear you sister. Try again."

I concentrated and then recited another number. Again I watched confusion parade across Gertie's face. "What is it?" I asked.

She held up a finger, listening intently to whomever was on the other end of the line. After a full thirty seconds, she hung up. She didn't even try to hide a grin. "Madame Zora the Psychic? Ohhh, the things I'm learning about you tonight."

"She's a client of mine," I said. "I'm trying to teach her to deliver her dour predictions with a bit more eloquence."

"Right, sure, that's a good story." Gertie's eyes twinkled merrily. "Gimmee another number. Let's see what else you've been up to in Boston."

I pressed my fingertips to my temples and tried to focus. Why hadn't I just programmed Cat's number in my contacts? "Okay, I've got it. I think." I gave her one more set of numbers.

Gertie's expression went from amused to stunned within seconds. She listened for a moment and then held out the phone for me to take. "It's for you."

With great trepidation, I took the phone and held it to my ear. I somehow managed to make myself speak. "Hello?"

"Good evening, Stephanie."

I gasped. It was Boris Sidorov.

Chapter Seven

I STARED STRAIGHT AHEAD as if mesmerized by a Moroccan snake charmer. I couldn't speak. Well, that's not technically true. I must have uttered some sort of strangled noise because Agent Mayeux and Carter broke off their conversation to stare at me.

"Boris?" I finally managed to squeak out. "Why do you have Cat's phone?"

"Because he killed her, duh," Gertie said in a stage whisper. "Find out where he is."

I turned away from her. Did she really think that Boris would tell me the truth about where he was? He was as experienced a liar as he was a murderer. My brain shouted out questions to ask him, but my tongue felt as if it were tied into a massive knot that made speech impossible. I glanced up to see Agent Mayeux and Carter coming toward me. In a matter of seconds they were going to yank my phone away from me. That realization loosed my tongue. "You're not going to get away with killing Cat," I told him. "Do you hear me, Boris? You're not."

"You needn't thank me, it was my pleasure." His laugh was cold and cruel, and it sent a shiver right down my spine. "You needn't fret. It's your turn next. Or maybe you would prefer I kill the blonde one next?"

"I don't understand. Who are you—" but before I could finish my question, Agent Mayeux snatched the phone from my hand and put it to his ear. In rapid succession he frowned, cursed, and held up the phone as if he wanted to throw it at the wall. "He hung up."

Carter groaned. "You think your guys will be able to get a trace on it?"

"Probably not. I'm sure the slime ball knows of a way to scramble the signal. But we'll check anyway." Agent Mayeux held the phone out. "Can you bag this for me while I call one of my guys to come get it?"

"You have guys? Here in Sinful?" I asked him as Carter whisked my cell phone away. "What are you going to do with my phone?"

"Analyze it so we can find out just who you've been talking to, as well as how often." His gaze was steely. "I didn't know you had Sidorov on speed dial."

"Don't be ridiculous. He's not on my speed dial. I don't even use speed dial."

"I'll vouch for that," Gertie chimed in. "All you're going to find on that phone are calls to the Jade Palace and Madame Zora. Craving egg foo young and trying to get a glimpse into the future aren't crimes, you know."

He stared at her for a long moment, a perplexed frown on his face. "What are you talking about?" When she merely shrugged, he turned his attention to me. "Who is Madame Zora? Where does she fit into the Sidorovs' organization?"

I struggled to think of just how to respond before Gertie could, but I was too slow. She beat me to it.

"Madame Zora is Stephanie's psychic." She shifted in her chair so she could see me better. "Hey, what did she say the last time you called her? Maybe that will give us a clue?"

I stood up and collected my handbag from the chair next to me, hoping that my actions didn't show my internal angst. Madame

Zora was my guilty little secret. Just because I was prim and proper didn't mean I wasn't curious. I squared my shoulders and gave them each what I hoped was a no-nonsense look. "I find it curious that the two of you are more interested in my personal life and whom I might occasionally call than in what Boris Sidorov had to say."

"What did he say?" they asked in unison.

Relieved that we were off the subject of my personal life, I blew out a long breath. "I asked him why he had Cat's phone, but he dodged that question by telling me that I was next in line to be murdered. Unless I preferred he kill the blonde one next."

"Who is 'the blonde one'? Someone in his organization?" Agent Mayeux asked.

Gertie had grown uncharacteristically still. "Do you think he means Fortune?"

Carter arrived just in time to hear the last bit of her question. "What about Fortune?" Worry was evident in his voice. "What did I miss?"

Agent Mayeux filled him in on Boris' cryptic message.

"Did he use Fortune's name specifically?" Carter asked me.

I replayed the conversation in my mind. "No, he just said 'the blonde one.'"

"I need to get over there and check on her." But Carter hadn't taken six steps before his phone rang. He glanced at caller ID and swore. "It's Celia."

Not that I approved of his profanity, but if anyone in Sinful warranted the use of an expletive, it was Celia.

We listened to his side of the conversation. Mostly it was Celia's one-way conversation with herself. Carter only managed a few yes's, no's, and a few attempts to stop Celia from coming to the Sheriff's Department. His scowl when the call ended made it clear that he'd lost the battle. Celia Arceneaux, a legend in her own mind, was on her way to gloat over Ida Belle's arrest.

Gertie got to her feet. "Carter, you go check on Fortune. Just deputize me or something right quick and I'll handle our faux mayor."

"Jeez, Gertie, how dumb do you think I am?" Carter shook his head. "You need to clear on out of here because you're only going to make things worse."

Gertie folded her arms over her chest. "Young man, I'm going to morph into your worst nightmare in the blink of an eye if you try to get rid of me. We both know that if I run interference with Celia there's a better chance of keeping her away from Ida Belle. Which means we have a better chance of keeping Ida Belle from committing a real murder."

The look on Carter's face was thunderous, but he didn't argue with her logic.

"What about Fortune?" I asked. "Isn't someone supposed to be monitoring her activity via her ankle bracelet?"

For a split second I thought I saw an emotion (extreme annoyance was my guess) flash across Agent Mayeux's face, but it was gone before I was sure. However, his next words left me with no doubt that my question irked him. "Miss St. James, I'm going to crawl out on a limb here and assume you've never worked in law enforcement?"

I shook my head.

"Has a court order ever been issued to fit you with an ankle monitoring system?"

Again, I shook my head.

"Then just perhaps," he said, "you might leave the detective work to me?"

I nodded as graciously as I could, in spite of my own extreme annoyance. "Certainly, Agent Mayeux. Please proceed."

And proceed we did, straight out of the Sheriff's Department and into his truck. We had the good fortune to miss Celia's arrival. I pitied poor Carter having to deal with a gloating Celia and a mischievous Gertie. No one could ever accuse that poor man of not earning his salary.

The ride over to Fortune's was swift and silent. Agent Mayeux parked across the street from her house. He switched off the engine and pulled out a tablet. After a few taps and a few swipes, he closed the cover. "Something's wrong."

"That's hardly news," I answered. "Our glamping trip was ruined, poor Cat is dead, Boris is gloating like the pig he is, and my sweet Priscilla is heaven only knows where. Yes, I'd most definitely agree that something is wrong."

"No, I mean something is wrong in there." He motioned toward the house with his head. "They're not able to pick up on any movement on Fortune's device."

"Maybe she's sleeping?" I suggested. The front porch light was on, and it looked like the light in the kitchen was on, but perhaps she'd conked out on the couch.

"Even when people sleep they tend to toss and turn somewhat, especially if they've just been fitted with a monitor. Let's go check it out."

He stepped out on to the street and crossed in front of the truck on his way to open my door. Unfortunately, or fortunately perhaps, his back was toward the house just as I realized that he was right.

Something was up, and that something was Fortune herself—moving at the speed of light as she stepped out of the house, vaulted over the front porch railing, and disappeared into the night.

"I have half a mind to leave you in this truck," Agent Mayeux grumbled as he stood holding the truck door open for me. "Quit your hemming and hawing and let's get a move on."

"But—"

"But nothing, get out."

I was not about to do anything of the sort. Not until I saw Fortune slip back into the house. What was she thinking? Never mind that, where was she going? I hadn't seen a sign of anyone else with her, and her movements didn't look forced or coerced. Which meant she likely left of her own free will. Lucky her, out there all alone in the darkness. I'd trade places with her in an instant. Sitting in a truck parked on the curb under a yellow street light with an F.B.I. agent staring holes into me wasn't my idea of fun. I bit my lip while I scrambled to think of something to say that would keep us away from Fortune's front door.

"I'm hungry," I blurted out.

"Tough. Get out of the truck." When I didn't, Agent Mayeux folded his arms over his chest and stared down at me.

"Why don't we drive over to Mudbug? I heard there's a diner that's open all night. Word on the street is that the burgers are killer." Word on the street? Killer burgers? I barely recognized the words coming out of my mouth, but desperate times called for desperate phrases.

"Ain't gonna happen."

"But what if I collapse while I'm in your custody? Surely that won't be worth all the paperwork you'd have to file to explain how you let me suffer."

"You can eat after we check on Fortune."

His parents should have named him Stonewall, not Kase. "Don't you have anything in your glove box?" I persisted. "Crackers and cheese? An old candy bar even?"

"Go ahead, open it up and look. When you're done scrounging around for food, do me a favor and hand me my handcuffs. Because if you don't get out of my truck this instant, I'm going to slap them on your wrists and arrest you for obstruction."

I cocked my head and thought. Maybe it wouldn't be such a bad thing if he had to drive me back to the Sheriff's Department. Right now the thought of being booked and tossed into a cell with Aunt Ida Belle sounded preferable to sitting here. "Handcuffs aren't necessary, Agent. I won't resist if you need to take me back downtown."

Instead of answering me, he reached in and all but yanked me out of the truck. He slammed the door shut without loosening his grip on my arm. I did my best to drag my feet but it didn't really work well on the asphalt. Fortunately, I had more luck once we reached the front lawn. But even digging my heels into the grass didn't deter my companion. Without saying a word he let go of my wrist, slipped his arm around my back, swept the other under my knees, and held me in his arms like a child before I could say "Merciful heavens".

I didn't bother to struggle as I knew I was out-muscled by well over one hundred pounds. But still, I had to at least try to keep him out of Fortune's house. "Wait," I cried as he carried me up the front porch steps. "We don't have a key. I'm sure Gertie has one in her purse." Lord knew she had one of everything else in there. "Let's drive back to the Sheriff's Department and get it."

"We don't need a key."

About this he was right. No sooner had he spoken the words than the door swung open. It was Ally, in a robe, her eyes wide as she looked from me to Agent Mayeux to the snake on his arm and then back at me.

"Good grief, Stephanie, what's going on?" She gasped. "Don't tell me you eloped!"

Chapter Eight

ELOPED? WITH FEDERAL Agent Kase Mayeux? He of few words and many scowls? I think not. "Don't be ridiculous, Ally."

There must have been something in the definitive way I phrased my denial, perhaps it was the word "ridiculous", that prompted Agent Mayeux to set me down none too gently. As soon as my feet touched the front porch, I took a step forward to put some distance between us. I could think better that way.

"Move aside, we need to come in."

Ally obeyed his command and stepped back into the foyer. I followed her into the house. Once the door was shut behind him, I made introductions.

"F.B.I. agent?" Ally's face registered her confusion. "Stephanie, why was he carrying you? Are you hurt?" After I reassured her I wasn't injured, she drew me into a hug. "I heard about Ida Belle's arrest. I'm sorry. Obviously someone really screwed up." Her expression when she looked at my companion was full of censure. "Everyone knows Ida Belle couldn't possibly hurt anyone."

I'm sure there were people in Sinful who would argue that point, but I was supposed to play the part of a frantically worried niece, so I merely nodded. "The whole evening has been such a nightmare, Ally. But we shouldn't be here, we'll come back in the morning. I'm sorry we disturbed you."

I made a move to open the door but Agent Mayeux shot out a restraining arm and blocked my escape attempt.

"We need to see Fortune." He looked around. "Where is she?"

"Upstairs in her room, asleep." Ally's words were uncharacteristically frosty. "I saw what you're making her wear on her ankle. Not cool."

"I'm not here to debate that. Where's her room?"

This time it was me who blocked his move. I slipped in front of him and stood on the bottom step of the staircase leading up to second floor. "You most certainly will not burst into a lady's room while she's asleep, Agent Mayeux. You wait here and I'll go up and check on her." Well, technically I'd be checking on her empty room and scrambling to make up an excuse to buy Fortune some time to get back from wherever it was she'd gone. "Ally, perhaps you'd be kind enough to offer this gentleman a cup of coffee while he waits?"

And then before he could protest, I tore up the stairs in a most unladylike fashion. Luckily, her door wasn't locked. I slipped in and locked it behind me. "Fortune," I called out just loudly enough to be heard. "Are you here?"

I suspected she wasn't, but a part of me held out great hope that I'd only imagined her earlier escape. I experienced a stab of annoyance. Fortune and I hadn't exactly hit it off when we'd met, but I chalked that up to us coming from very different worlds. But if her shenanigans tonight ended up making things worse for my aunt, I was going to have it out with her.

My eyes scanned her bedroom. It was devoid of all of the frippery that I'd have expected of a former beauty queen. It was also devoid of Fortune. I groaned aloud when I heard Agent Mayeux's raised voice draw nearer. I looked around frantically. Where would Fortune have left her tracking device? The closet. I threw open the closet doors and ran my hands through the few things on hangers but I didn't feel anything. Fortune's shoe shelf held a single pair of high heels and the rest were athletic shoes. One glance assured me that she hadn't hidden her ankle monitor here.

I didn't have a moment to spare so I turned to her undergarment drawer. Despite the obvious impropriety, I yanked open the top drawer and swept my hands through her unmentionables. Bingo. I pulled out what looked like one of those collars dogs wear to prevent them from barking. It was made of a heavy black plastic and had a beeping red light.

The door handle rattled. My heart hammered in my chest. I didn't know who to blame for the predicament I found myself in, Fortune or Boris Sidorov. But I could assign blame later. Right now I had to deal with an angry F.B.I. agent.

"Open the door, Miss St. James."

"Just a moment, please," I called out. I ran over to the window and hoisted it open. The smell of swamp water assailed my nose as the night air blew into the room. I knew from previous visits that the bayou ran behind Fortune's house. Was it too far for me to pitch the ankle monitor into the water? Was that even the right thing to do? How would Fortune explain that when she got back?

Agent Mayeux pounded on the door. "Open up or I'll kick this thing in."

"I truly have to question your understanding of southern manners, Agent." I had to shout to be heard over the pounding. "Please just exercise a tiny bit of patience."

Expecting him to do nothing of the kind, I decided that my only hope was to dispose of the ankle monitor. Fortune could explain her way out of it—after all, she was the one who was supposed to be wearing the darn thing. I leaned out of the window, hoping to be able to see just how far I had to pitch it.

"Psst, Stephanie, down here."

Startled, I glanced down. Fortune stood just under the window. I didn't know if I was relieved to see her or supremely annoyed. Probably a good mixture of both.

"Hold on," she called in a stage whisper. "I'm coming up."

"There' s no time." Agent Mayeux was going to pop a vein if he caught Fortune climbing in the window. I held out the ankle monitor. "Catch this and then find a way to get in the house."

Agent Mayeux's voice thundered through the door. "I'm going to count to five. If you don't unlock this door, I'm busting it down. One."

I had no time to wait for Fortune to agree. "Heads up." And then I dropped it straight down. How that would look on the F.B.I.'s monitoring system, I had no idea. Frankly, at this point, I didn't care.

"Two."

"Don't you dare kick down that door," I yelled as I slid the window closed. "I'll be right there."

"Three."

I glanced down into the darkened yard but didn't see Fortune. "I'm coming." I ran over to the door just as he reached the count of four. I unlocked it and stepped back. "You may enter now."

Ignoring me completely, he barreled into the room.

I swept my arm out. "As you can see, Fortune isn't in here. Maybe she's having a shower."

Agent Mayeux glowered at me. "No one's in the bathroom. I checked."

"Well then, I hardly know what to think."

Instead of acknowledging my comment, he strode through the room. After a cursory examination, he turned to me. "Where is she?"

I shrugged. "How would I know? I've been with you all evening. Did you ask Ally before you tore up here?"

Before he could answer, Fortune appeared in the doorway, wearing an innocent smile along with her ankle monitor. "Hi guys," she said, looking between us. "I was out in the garage getting a cold beer. Care to join me?"

AS WE SAT AROUND FORTUNE'S kitchen table, I had to admit the woman was smooth. She'd commandeered the conversation from the get go and hadn't relinquished control for a second despite the barrage of questions.

"Are you sure you wouldn't like a beer to wash that sandwich down?" Fortune asked.

Agent Mayeux, in the process of scarfing down his second turkey and avocado sandwich, shook his head. At least he had the good manners not to speak with his mouth full. He, like every other person in Sinful, appeared powerless to resist Ally's cooking. I myself was nibbling on my fourth chocolate chip cookie.

"Since you're here, Agent Mayeux, perhaps you could look at my ankle monitor?" Fortune glanced down at it, her expression the epitome of innocence. "I'm not sure it's working correctly. It's been making funny little sounds."

I made a funny little sound of my own as I choked on a mouthful of cookie.

Ally reached over and thumped my back. "Easy does it, Stephanie. Let me get you another glass of milk."

I smiled my gratitude. I was fast coming to adore Ally. She was a lovely person. So uncomplicated and easy to be with. Unlike Fortune.

"Tell me how Ida Belle's holding up," Fortune said. "I've been worrying like crazy about her."

"She's locked up in a cell for a crime she didn't commit. How do you think she is?" As soon as the words were out of my mouth, I cringed at how curt I sounded. Fortune was just playing her part in front of Ally. "I'm sorry."

Fortune waved her hand. "Don't be. We're all overwrought."

His sandwich devoured, Agent Mayeux pushed away his plate. "Tell me what you know about Boris Sidorov."

"Me? Nothing," Fortune said. "Just what I've heard about him from Stephanie. Why do you ask?"

"You've never met him?"

"No."

I shot a sideways look at her. The way she lied without hesitation was downright unnerving. But in fairness, I'd seen Gertie and Aunt Ida Belle do the same.

I decided to jump in and see if we could move this conversation along. "Do you know who 'the blonde one' is?"

A small frown settled between Fortune's eyebrows. "The blonde one? Is that some sort of code?"

"Yes, Boris said he was going to kill me unless I preferred 'the blonde one' die next," I hurried to answer before Agent Mayeux could speak. "We thought he might have meant you."

"Whoa, hold on a minute." Fortune made a time out sign with her hands. "When did you talk to Boris? What else did he say?"

I realized then that she hadn't heard the story of our visit to the morgue, so I filled her in. I had to choke back tears when I told her about Cat. Ally reached over and laid a sympathetic hand on my shoulder. I smiled my thanks.

"If you're quite finished, Miss St. James, I'll take over from here."

I nodded. "You may have the floor."

He then proceeded to question, no, make that interrogate, Fortune. But if she knew any of the answers to his questions, she wasn't giving anything up. His frustration was palpable. Perhaps I should have felt sorry for him. After all, he'd been exposed to Gertie, Aunt Ida Belle, and Fortune all in one night. That was a lot for any man to handle.

A short while later, when Agent Mayeux was looking at Fortune's ankle monitor to see why it was malfunctioning, I asked Ally if I could have a private word with her in the hallway.

Her expression was full of concern as she waited for me to speak.

"I know this might sound like a crazy question," I began, "but have you ever heard anything through the grapevine about Fortune's line of work before she arrived in Sinful?"

Ally cocked her head as she considered my question. "Are you talking about her pageant career or her work as a librarian?"

"Neither." I glanced over my shoulder to make sure that Fortune couldn't hear us. "I'm talking about her time in the C.I.A.."

Ally didn't try to hide her amusement, but at least she didn't laugh out loud. "C.I.A.? As in the Central Intelligence Agency?" She giggled. "I don't know who told you that but they were just messing with you. You know, making fun of the new girl in town."

I forced myself to smile. "You're probably right. Forget I said anything, and please don't tell Fortune. I'd feel so foolish."

"Of course, it's already forgotten."

We rejoined the others in the kitchen.

"Find out anything about the monitor?" Ally asked. "I think it's really insane that you're even having her wear it. Can't you at least let her take it off at night?"

"No."

If Ally was offended by his curt reply, she hid it well. "Are you two heading back to the jail now?"

I looked at Agent Mayeux. I had no idea what we were doing next, but surely he must.

"No."

I was quickly beginning to believe that the government had a low threshold for the verbal part of the F.B.I. entrance exam.

"Well, if no one objects, I'm going to go upstairs, throw on some clothes, and take some food to Ida Belle and Gertie," Ally said.

Before Agent Mayeux could object, or I could tell her what a lovely gesture I thought that was, Fortune pronounced that this was a brilliant idea. She did so with such gusto that I was suspicious. Why was she so anxious to see Ally leave?

Not long after she'd gone, Agent Mayeux indicated we were going to leave.

"Not without trying some of Ally's world class chocolate cookies, you're not," Fortune protested. "You don't know how long of a night it's going to be, so you might as well be well fortified."

"Wrap them up to go."

"Nonsense." Fortune put a handful of cookies on a small plate. She set them on the table in front of him and then poured him a glass of milk. "Here you go, something to wash them down with." She turned toward me. "Do you want any more cookies, Stephanie?"

"No, thank you." I sat back down beside Agent Mayeux. He made short work of the cookies and then drained his glass of milk. But after he wiped his mouth and set his napkin aside, he didn't immediately get up. Instead he frowned and then shook his head from side to side a few times. He blinked rapidly as if he was trying to focus on Fortune, who was sitting across from him. My eyes widened in alarm as he began to lean toward me.

"It's okay. I've got him." Fortune was up and out of her chair in a flash. She grabbed hold of him just before he toppled into my lap. I watched in horror as she eased him back into a sitting position and then gently leaned him forward so his head rested on the table.

I jumped to my feet. "I'll call 911."

She reached out and grabbed my arm. "Don't you dare. He's fine. He just needs to sleep it off."

Okay, that was it. She had officially lost her mind. This time I was sure of it. "Sleep what off? Cookies and milk?"

She pulled me around the table before she let go of my arm. "I promise you that he's fine. He'll just be out awhile. Now, if you have to use the bathroom before we go, get a move on."

"Go where?" Panic had turned my tone of voice into a decidedly unladylike shriek. "We can't leave him like this! And just where do you think you're going with that thing still around your ankle?" But no sooner had I finished the sentence than she was holding it in her hands. I stared incredulously. "How did you do that?"

She opened the pantry and tossed it on the cereal shelf. "A little trick I picked up."

"Where? On the beauty pageant circuit?"

But she didn't answer because she was too busy man-handling Agent Mayeux. My mind raced with questions as I watched her rifle though his pockets—no easy task considering how fitted his jeans were.

I gasped as the last piece of the puzzle fell into place. "Fortune, you drugged him, didn't you?"

She stopped rifling through his pockets and looked up at me. "Sometimes it's impossible to believe that you and Ida Belle are related."

"But what about—"

She held up his truck keys triumphantly. "Got 'em. Let's go."

"We're going to steal his truck?" I backed away in horror. "Surely that's some sort of federal offense? No way. I'm not going to prison. Not for you, not for anybody. That's grand theft, isn't it? I think that's a felony."

"Calm down, we're not stealing anything," Fortune said. "We're just going to hide the keys in case he wakes up. It'll slow him down, not hurt him." She pulled out the garbage can from under the sink and dropped the keys into it. She then gave it a good shake so the keys would be covered in rubbish before she put it away. "Let's go."

"How? Where?" I didn't have a chance to get to "why" before she propelled me out of the back door and down toward the bayou.

"But—but—" I tried to string together an objection but before I could, she pushed me onto a waiting airboat.

My protests were drowned out by the sound of the engine roaring to life.

Fortune turned back to look at me. "You'd better buckle up, Stephanie. Things might get a little crazy from here on out."

Chapter Nine

FORTUNE SPED THROUGH the night as if the hounds of hell were on our heels. The darkness was so pervasive that I lost what little bearings I had. What time was it? How much longer before the sun would come up? I didn't dare let go of my seat long enough to sneak a look at my watch. I shouted my question, but Fortune either didn't hear me or was ignoring me. Probably the latter.

She had to know that I had a million questions for her. Topping the list was where were we going. Why couldn't she have gone alone and left me on land? What if Ally came back to the house and found a drugged federal agent slumped over the kitchen table? Oh, yes, let me add this doozy to the list: did she know that we were likely going to end up incarcerated once we were caught?

I was on number twenty-six of a long list of questions I wanted answers to when the boat began to slow. My relief slowly gave way to revulsion as a stench of...I couldn't even say it out loud...reached my nostrils. I released my tight grip on my seat and covered my nose and mouth with my hands.

Fortune glanced over her shoulder at me. "Pretty horrible, isn't it?"

I nodded emphatically but didn't risk speaking because that would have required inhaling tainted oxygen. It wasn't going to happen. I'd rather pass out.

"It's Number Two," she told me. "That's the name of the island." She motioned for me to come and join her up front.

Reluctantly, I did. By this time we had slowed considerably. The night was still. I'm not sure a word like "quiet" could ever be applied to any part of the Louisiana bayou. Plenty of assorted critters contributed to creating an ambient backdrop of sounds that, quite frankly, unnerved me. I wasn't even fond of the sound of crickets through a screened window five stories off the ground. My pesky dependence on oxygen required me to drop my hands and inhale. I did—and promptly gagged.

"Just try not to focus on it," Fortune said. "You'll get a little more used to it."

"Never," I managed to choke out. "Why are we here?"

She looked around, although at what I couldn't fathom. The sounds and smells were overwhelming. The view, not so much.

"I received a tip that Boris is hiding out here."

Among the foul stench in gator filled waters? I thought not. "You don't know him, Fortune. He's, well, he's soft. He likes his creature comforts. He's certainly not the rugged outdoor type. If he's still here in Louisiana, I'm sure he's in a luxurious penthouse suite in New Orleans."

She shook her head. "No, my source is rock solid reliable. If they tell me that Sidorov is here, he's here."

Her source? She said this as if getting a tip to the location of a dangerous Russian mob boss were a normal part of her life. No sooner had I processed that thought than alarm bells begin to ring in my mind. I took a step backward. Fortune was a C.I.A. agent. In her own mind. This was my first up-close experience with someone who was clinically delusional. It certainly wasn't an experience I wished to prolong.

"I don't like that look on your face, Stephanie." Fortune frowned. "I need you to hold it together."

Me? I wasn't the one who had lost touch with my true identity. I was Stephanie St. James, Miss Prim and Proper, and I belonged in a building. With doors. Not in a floating tin can in a murky swamp. To my utter shock, I realized that the person I wanted beside me right now more than anyone else in the world was Kase Mayeux. He wasn't friendly, he wasn't especially charming, but he was made of tough stuff. He had to be if he'd endured having that huge snake tattooed into his skin. And then a chilling thought occurred to me. "Did you kill Kase?"

"Kase? You mean Agent Mayeux? No, of course not. I just gave him a little something to drift off. He'll wake up in a few hours and then the only thing that will be wrong with him is that he'll be angry that he slept through the fun."

The fun? I swallowed hard. Now I found myself wishing that she'd laced my milk, too. I'd much rather be asleep at the kitchen table than here in the most foul smelling place on earth. "Can we go back and check on him?" I suggested. "In fact, why not leave me there at the house? I can handle things when he wakes up."

She stared at me a long moment. "You're afraid, I get that."

Yes, I was. Afraid of her. But what was I supposed to say? Not the truth. I don't think my options had ever been more limited. It wasn't like I could swim for the shore. I couldn't even see the shore. Not to mention the filthy water, and then there was the whole issue of gators. Clearly, I was sticking with Fortune until I was back on land. Heaven help me, I would just have to play along.

"Why are we stopped?" I asked.

"I just wanted a moment to fill you in before we get to the island."

"Island?"

"Number Two."

Our conversation was starting to feel like a game of "who's on first". I wanted to weep with frustration, but the thought of Aunt Ida Belle sitting in the Sinful Jail kept my tears at bay. She was doing her part, so I had to do mine. It was too late to help poor Catriona, but Boris had to be found so he could be held accountable. But I'd bet my pearls he would never come near a place like this, even if Fortune's imaginary source told her otherwise. I didn't know what else to do but play along until she tired of this charade and wanted to go back home. "If you're sure he's here, why not call Carter and let law enforcement handle his arrest?"

"I can't do that," she said. Her voice sounded a tad forlorn. "Believe me, I wish I could."

"I see. So, let me get this straight. You have intentionally left a capable sheriff's deputy out of the loop and you've sedated an F.B.I. agent, all because you believe you and I are the ones who should capture a known criminal. Have I got that right?"

Fortune nodded. "You've got it." She surveyed the darkness. "We'd better get a move on before there's any sign of daylight. Just follow my lead and do exactly as I say. Don't improvise, don't hesitate, and don't give in to fear."

Without a word I retook my seat, because really, what was there to say? I sat quietly as Fortune guided the boat through the darkness. Roughly ten minutes later she slowed down until we were barely moving. Just what she was looking for, I didn't know, but somehow she found it. She took a long aluminum rod from the boat's floor and stuck it into the swampy water. We must have been near enough to land that it hit bottom because she managed to pull us close to shore. After she secured the boat to a low-hanging tree branch, she beckoned for me to stand beside her.

"Stay right behind me, Stephanie. Just be my shadow until we get to the cabin," she said in a whisper so low I wasn't sure if she was really speaking or if I was imagining it.

"But what about alligators?"

"We're okay, I've got a gun."

Somehow this didn't reassure me, but I jumped off right after she did. Fortune grabbed hold of my hand and pulled me along beside her as we moved ahead. I didn't resist because it was too dark for me to see on my own, and she had a gun. It took all I had not to gag from the stench of the island. This, I realized, was truly the lowest point of my life. I was at rock bottom.

Fortune continued dragging me along as if I were a limp rag doll. I was glad we were moving at the pace we were because it kept me from sinking into the squishy, muddy terrain. So focused was I on moving that when Fortune stopped, I bumped into her. "Sorry."

She shook her head furiously and held a finger to her lips. Once I nodded my understanding, she pointed and I gazed in that direction. A yellow light glowed from a square window. My eyes widened. A window! There was civilization on this most foul piece of swampy land.

Fortune's tension was palpable as we approached the cabin. She stopped every few steps to assess the situation. Or maybe she was having second thoughts every few steps. All I knew was that if she decided to tuck tail and run, I'd be right behind her. But she pressed forward until the cabin was about thirty feet away. She crouched down low and motioned for me to do the same.

I could smell cigarette smoke before I could see the person who was smoking. My breath caught in my throat. I recognized the scent from my visits to the Sidorov's home—it was a Russian cigarette. I did my best to convey this to Fortune by miming it. She nodded her understanding. Delusional she might be, but she was also sharp. I'd give her that.

"Wait here," she whispered. She reached into her waistband and pulled out a gun. "Don't move."

I didn't want to move, but neither did I want to stay. Which would I rather face? An alligator or an angry Sidorov? I decided it was a draw. I watched as Fortune crept forward, moving with the stealth of a panther. As she grew closer to the glowing cigarette light, I held my breath. Just what did she think she was going to do? Ask politely if she'd reached the Sidorovs' summer residence?

But apparently words weren't needed. Fortune came up behind the man, a bodyguard I assumed, and cracked him over the head with her gun. He crumpled and hit the ground. She circled the house and then motioned for me to join her under the window. I made my way over, grateful not to be alone any longer. I cast an uneasy glance at the bodyguard as I stepped over him. Maybe this little incident would impress upon him the dangers of smoking.

Like Lucy and Ethel in an '*I Love Lucy*' episode, Fortune and I held onto the window ledge and rose in unison to take a peek inside.

I somehow managed not to gasp when I saw the man who sat in a chair in front of the fireplace. He was sitting at an angle that didn't allow me to see his face, but I'd recognize that shiny dome of a bald head anywhere. It was Boris Sidorov.

The sight of him disgusted me. And then disgust gave way to shock. I struggled to take a deep breath. Sitting on Boris' lap was a white Persian cat. My white Persian cat. He had Priscilla. The bastard.

I shot to my feet. Fortune reached out to grab my arm, but I shook her off and ran toward the front of the cabin. It was time for Boris Sidorov to be taken down, and I was the crazed cat owner who was going to do it.

Chapter Ten

MY RIGHTEOUS ANGER carried me just far enough for me to burst through the cabin door. But once I was inside, my bravado deserted me. I had no idea what to say or do next.

"Close the damn door, Vasily." Boris didn't bother to turn around to make sure that it was actually his bodyguard who stood there. "This place stinks to hell and back."

When I didn't answer, he let loose a litany of Russian swear words and shifted in his chair. The look on his face when he saw me would have been comical, if I hadn't scared out of my mind.

"Miss St. James, what a surprise," he finally said.

I ignored him. "Come here, Priscilla, darling," I called to her. She leapt off of Boris' lap before he could grab hold of her, but she didn't come toward my outstretched arms. Instead, she sauntered right past me and jumped up on top of a rifle cabinet. She looked down at me with fire in her gorgeous green eyes. Oh, she was mad, but I didn't blame her. The poor thing had been cooped up with Boris on this smelly island for heaven only knew how long. She was going to make me pay for that.

Speaking of paying, Catriona was the one who had lost her life. Now Boris had to pay.

Boris stood but didn't make a move toward me. Yet. I knew he was trying to assess the situation. Likely he was wondering where Vasily was—I know I was certainly wondering where in the world

Fortune had disappeared to. "Come here, little blonde one," he called to Priscilla. She blinked and looked away.

Little blonde one? So it was Priscilla he had threatened to kill next, not Fortune? I'd never been more disgusted in my life. What kind of a man threatened to kill an innocent cat?

Seeing that he was getting zero response from her, he turned his attention to me. "Did you come alone?"

I hesitated. What was the right answer to that? I was so in over my head. What on earth had prompted me to burst in there like I was a character in an action adventure movie? As much as I hated to admit it, I'd pulled a Gertie by acting first and thinking later. Sinful was getting to me, and obviously not in a good way. "Of course, I didn't come alone. I brought a highly trained C.I.A. operative with me," I lied.

Boris scoffed at that. "The C.I.A.? What a bunch of incompetent morons. You'd have been better off to have brought the old ladies along with you as back up."

And there was the only thing in the entire world that Boris Sidorov and I would ever agree on.

"I wouldn't let her hear you say that, Boris." Not that she was anywhere around, but I didn't know what else to do but bluff.

"Her? You brought a woman to deal with me?" He laughed so hard that he snorted. "Surely this is a joke."

"Cat's dead because of you, Boris. That's no joke." I could feel anger in my core beginning to rise like lava out of a volcano. I was going to blow. "You killed her. And you're not going to get away with it."

He took a step toward me, his eyes locked on mine. "That cat woman doesn't matter."

I choked on my rage. "Yes, she did. Why did you have to kill her?"

He shrugged. "I wanted the blonde one. She wouldn't give it to me."

Where was Fortune? Surely she hadn't absconded and left me to fend for myself? I could only hope that I looked calmer on the outside than I felt on the inside. I had to keep Boris talking until I could figure out what to do next. "Why did you want Priscilla?"

"I figured if I dismembered your precious cat, piece by piece, it would be a small start in making you pay for what you did to my two sons."

My eyes shot up to where Priscilla lay sprawled out. I could see four paws, two eyes, and her tail. Thank God. "What I did to your sons? You're the reason Misha is dead and Vladimir is locked up, Boris. You had to know that your criminal lifestyle was going to corrupt your sons." His face was turning purple. Good. Goading him was working. With any luck, he'd have a fit and drop dead at my feet. "You babied your precious Misha so much that he couldn't take no for an answer when I refused to marry him."

"You weren't good enough for him," Boris spat out. "You're a stupid, cheap whore."

"So you hired me, a stupid, cheap whore, to teach your sons manners? That hardly indicates that you had a high opinion of them," I taunted him. "You favored Misha so much that you drove Vladimir to kill him in a desperate attempt to get your attention. The blood's on your hands, Boris. Not mine."

I watched as he growled and flexed his fingers. I took this as both a good and bad sign. The growl was good because it meant I was getting to him. But it was bad that he was flexing his fingers. He was going to strangle me.

"So you killed Catriona? For once, why don't you be a man and admit it?"

Boris' face flushed four shades of red. "Don't be stupid. Of course I am a man. A great man. I killed Catriona Carmichael. Are you happy now?"

Happy? No. But I did find it utterly fascinating that the way to make a Russian mob boss confess to murder was to question his manhood. "No. I'm not happy," I told him. I wasn't happy that Catriona was dead. I wasn't happy that Fortune had deserted me. And I was most especially unhappy that I had no idea what to say or do next to get out of this situation alive.

"That's a shame," Boris said, taking yet another step toward me. He flexed his fingers, his eyes fixed on my neck.

I reached up and touched my pearls. Images of the bruises I'd seen on Catriona's neck paraded through my mind.

"It's your time to die, Miss Prim and Proper." Boris smiled. Apparently my showing up, unarmed and with no plan, had made his day.

"Not today, it's not."

Boris wheeled around. My eyes widened as I watched Fortune walk through a door at the back of the cabin. She had a gun trained on Boris' head. "On your knees, Sidorov," she commanded. "Now."

Her voice was pure steel. She didn't sound like the Fortune I'd come to know. Her hand that held the gun was steady and her body looked ready to spring into action. She completely looked the part of a trained member of a federal law enforcement bureau. I had no idea those beauty pageants trained their contestants to be such superb actresses.

Boris pivoted slowly. Clearly, he'd been caught off guard. But the fact that he hadn't done what Fortune ordered made it clear he didn't perceive her as much of a threat.

"Last warning, Sidorov. Down on your knees."

He opened his mouth to either protest or to mock her, I never learned which. Before he was able to say a word, Fortune pulled the trigger and fired off two shots.

Boris screamed. I think I saw blood. I know I saw a streak of white fur flash past me as Priscilla bolted out the front door. I believe Fortune pulled out a pair of handcuffs, but I'm not entirely certain because that was the point I fainted and hit the floor in what I'm afraid was a most unladylike fashion.

"COME ON, STEPHANIE, you have to eat something."

I forced myself to look at Gertie. Her concern for my welfare was clear to see in her eyes, much the same as I saw in my Aunt Ida Belle's expression when she looked at me. "I can't eat, Gertie. But I'm okay, really I am."

"Hogwash and slop, you're okay." She set the plate on the coffee table, but she didn't move from where she'd perched on the edge of the couch. "Now tell Auntie Gertie just what's bothering you. Because you know Fortune had to shoot Boris, don't you?"

I pulled the blanket up under my chin. "I know she did."

"Are you upset that she didn't kill him?" Gertie persisted. "She thought death was too good for him, and I don't disagree with her. He can sit and rot in prison for the rest of his life for all I care." She chuckled. "He's going to hate it."

I frowned. "Either way, Catriona's not coming back. If Boris died or stays in prison, it doesn't change that."

She laid a gentle hand on my knee. "I know, honey. I know. But you aren't responsible for what Boris did. The loss of your friend is one of those horrible, unfair things that happens in life that we can't control. You can find a way to honor her life, maybe something to do with helping homeless cats or something. But you gotta go on."

I nodded. Gertie was right. Aunt Ida Belle had said much the same thing several times in the last two days. The previous forty-eight hours had been an absolute whirlwind of activity and endless questions. I was just beginning to sort everything out in my mind.

"Now, let's focus on something positive. Not only is your aunt out of jail but she's a local hero for helping Carter lull old Boris into a sense of false security. That's probably why he wasn't carrying a gun when you stormed in on him." She flashed a wide smile. "You want to hear the story of how Celia had to eat crow when she had to give Ida Belle an official commendation for assisting the Sheriff's Department?"

This was a story I'd already heard. As proud as I was of my aunt, five times was enough for me. Gertie would be getting mileage out of this story for months, if not years, to come. I was saved from having to hear it again by Fortune, who appeared holding a plate of brownies.

"Go on, Gertie. It's my turn to pester Stephanie." She waited until Gertie had gone off, brownie in hand, before she set the remaining ones on the table beside the sandwich Gertie had brought in. She plopped down on the floor beside the couch and drew her knees up to her chest.

"Seems like we've got some things to straighten out, don't we?"

"Such as?" I asked. I didn't know where she was going with this. I'd thanked her, quite sincerely, several times for saving me from the same fate that Cat had met. She'd explained to me in great detail how she'd studied martial arts in her pre-pageant days. Just how she'd known the best way to knock out Vasliy with one blow or how to shoot Boris in the thigh so that he was incapacitated and not dead, she didn't elaborate on. But I didn't press her. Why bother? She'd just come up with another tale that had little basis in reality. She seemed downright relieved that I didn't question any part of her story, including how she'd managed to contact Carter so that he could show up and arrest Boris and Vasily while she and I slipped back to the house. "I think we've covered everything."

"You know I had to take you along when I went looking for Boris, right?" she asked. "We needed a confession, and you were the only one able to provoke one out of him."

I nodded. "I understand. I'm glad if it helped."

"It did." Fortune watched me for a long moment before she spoke again. "So, you're good? Willing to let it all go?"

I nodded.

"No loose ends, no last questions?" she persisted.

I almost nodded again but caught myself. "Just one question. Are you certain, one hundred percent certain, that we're not in trouble for drugging Kase?"

"We're clear," Fortune confirmed. "He's not happy about it, but the word has come down from his superiors that there won't be any follow-up to his claim that he was drugged. As far as they're concerned, he fell asleep on the job."

"But he didn't."

"No, he didn't."

"Then why are we hanging him out to dry?" This wasn't so easy to let go of. Boris could pay the piper, I didn't care what fate awaited him. I was done with the Sidorovs for good. End of that story. My guilt over what happened to Cat would stay with me forever, but Gertie was right. I could find a way to honor Cat's memory. But letting Agent Mayeux face censure for something he wasn't guilty of, that wasn't okay. "It's not right."

"In our line of work—" she stopped and corrected herself, "—in his line of work, things don't always end up in pretty little packages. He won't lose his job and this won't be held against him. It's complicated."

"You seem awfully concerned about that fellow." Aunt Ida Belle plopped in the chair across from me. She studied me thoughtfully. "Anything happen between you two while I was in lock-up that I should know about?"

"Of course not," I protested. "The man's nothing but a nuisance."

"A nuisance with a cute butt," Gertie called from the window. "Speak of the devil, here comes Agent Hunky now."

I struggled to a sitting position and whipped the blanket off my knees. I wasn't about to be caught lounging around like an invalid. Thankfully I'd rejected the sweatpants and t-shirt that Aunt Ida Belle had offered me to wear this morning in favor of a mint green sundress. I only hoped that the half-dozen baths I'd taken since my return from Number Two had done away with the stench. I'd scrubbed with salt, sugar, and bathed in every scent of bath bombs that Walter's store carried. I reached up to make sure my French braid was intact.

"You look fine," Fortune said. She got to her feet. "I'm going to duck out back and have a beer. Care to join me, girls?"

With a wry smile, Aunt Ida Belle got up and dragged Gertie away from the window. "Come on, you old fool, he's not the first man with six pack abs that you've ever seen and he's not going to be the last. Let's leave the young ones to talk."

I was grateful to be alone because if they talked like that in front of Kase, I'd die of embarrassment.

"Hello, Agent Mayeux," I said as I pulled open the front door. "Won't you come in?"

He stared down at me a long moment. I didn't look away. Something about him was different from the last time I'd seen him. Maybe it was because he'd changed out his black t-shirt for a navy blue one, or maybe it was something else. I don't know. And it didn't really matter. This would likely be the last time I'd ever see him. No doubt they were sending him back to New Orleans.

"I'd rather sit here outside." He gestured toward the front porch steps. "If you don't mind?"

"Of course not." Obviously he was afraid to set foot inside the same house as me. I didn't offer him anything to eat or drink. He'd probably think I was going to drug him again. I sat down on the top step, settled my dress over my knees, and folded my hands in my lap. I waited to speak until he sat beside me. "Are you here to ask about the cookies and milk again?"

"No."

I waited but he didn't say anything else.

"Then may I ask why you dropped by?" We both knew it wasn't to be social.

He took off his aviator sunglasses and let them dangle from one hand. "I just spoke to LeBlanc. They're done on Number Two."

Tears pricked the back of my eyes. I knew why he was telling me this. If the Sheriff's Department was done processing the cabin as a crime scene, there was no need for anyone to be on the island. Which meant that the likelihood of anyone finding Priscilla alive was next to none. My sweet girl was going to end up as a gator snack. I could only hope that the alligator who ate her choked on her fur and died. "Thank you for telling me."

He nodded. "You miss her?"

"I do." More than I could even put into words. I hadn't said much in front of Aunt Ida Belle, Gertie, or Fortune about Priscilla. If they knew how much I adored my cat they'd think I was crazy. They wouldn't understand. "The funny thing is, I swear I can hear her precious little meow right now." The sound was obviously going to haunt me forever. I stood. "Well, I guess this is goodbye."

"It's not. Sit down."

Oh, what this man didn't know about the power of the word *'please'*. But I sat. I owed him that much. He had to be beyond irritated and aggrieved about the "Great Sedation by Milk and Cookies" incident, as Gertie had taken to calling it.

"I'm not leaving town just yet," he said. "Neither are you."

My eyebrows rose. "I haven't decided what my plans are."

"I have." He turned and leaned back against the porch railing so he could better see me. "I've been given some time off, so to speak, by my department. I'm sure you understand why."

I nodded sheepishly.

"I thought I'd stick around Sinful. There've been some rumors of drug runners moving into the area, and I want to do some poking around on my own. Maybe I can find out a thing or two that will help me out with my superiors. I'd like to do what I can to save my reputation before I'm forever known around the office as Agent Sleepy."

I winced. "But what does that have to do with me?" I asked.

"One of the suspects is throwing a big wedding for his niece next weekend. I've wrangled an invitation. But I need to fly under the radar, so to speak."

I couldn't help but smile. How did a man with a massive snake tattooed around his upper body think he was going to fly under anyone's radar? "I see."

"I need a date for the wedding."

I waited for him to say more but he stayed silent. "You want me to find a date for you?"

He shook his head. "You're my date for the wedding."

I stared at him. He had to be kidding.

"I'm serious."

"Maybe you are, but that doesn't mean I have to agree."

It was his turn to smile. "Actually, there are two very good reasons why you might want to reconsider. The first is that I'm going to be much more likely to forgive you for your part in humiliating me if you help me out."

"You'd be willing to forgive and forget?" Frankly, that was a tad more generous than I'd have been under the circumstances.

"I forget nothing. But I might forgive you."

"And the second reason I should consider posing as your date?"

"I have something I think you want."

I frowned. Surely he wasn't...no, he wouldn't speak to a lady like that. Would he? I was half afraid to ask. "Such as?"

He glanced toward his truck parked out on the street. "Agree to be my date for the wedding and I'll show you."

I blew out a long breath. What to do, what to do? A part of me was anxious to leave Sinful behind and get back to my life in Boston where things were a little more prim and proper. On the other hand, I found myself curiously attached to my aunt and

Gertie. I even thought I could grow to like Fortune over time, although that depended on how out of control her delusions got. On top of that, I owed Agent Mayeux something for my part in embarrassing him in front of his colleagues. After all, it was one wedding and one reception. One evening. It couldn't be any more difficult than the night in the bayou I'd just been survived."Okay, I'll do it."

He nodded, looking awfully self-satisfied with himself. "Stay here, I'll be right back."

I watched as he jogged to his truck. I'm embarrassed to admit that I completely agreed with Gertie. The man had a fine posterior. But as he headed back toward me, my thoughts of his physique flew out of my mind. Instead, I stared at the fluffy white bundle in his arms.

I shot to my feet and ran down the steps to meet him. I hardly dared hope. "Priscilla?"

He held her out to me and I gratefully took her. I held her up so I could look into her beautiful emerald eyes. It was her! My sweet baby girl was alive and well. I hugged her to me and nuzzled my face in her fur. She allowed me to love on her for a moment but then squirmed out of my arms and sauntered over to the front steps where she sat and stared at the door.

"It looks like she's not very happy with you," he said.

That comment showed how little he knew about cats. It wasn't about a cat loving you. It was about a cat condescending to let you love it. He must be a dog man. I smiled up at him. "How can I ever thank you?"

"Just help me out at the wedding. And don't even think about slipping anything into my food or drink. I'll be watching you like a hawk."

That was an unsettling thought. But never mind, it was worth it to have Priscilla back with me. And then another thought occurred to me. "Wait, why does she smell so good? You found her on Number Two, right?"

He shrugged. "We stopped at the groomer's on the way over."

I didn't try to hide my delight. "Thank you." I touched my heart. "Really, thank you. I promise to be the perfect date for the wedding. Just tell me when it is and I'll be ready."

He took a few steps toward me. "I'll pick you up at eight tomorrow morning."

He was close enough now that I had to tilt my head back in order to see his face. "Tomorrow? I thought you said the wedding was next weekend."

He shook his head. "The wedding's not until then, but I told you I want to fly under the radar, not stick out. So I'm going to spend the week in Sinful being seen out and about with my girl—that's you by the way—while I start poking around."

Before I knew what he was about to do, he leaned down and brushed a kiss across my cheek. "Just in case anyone is watching," he said in a low voice. He jogged back to his truck and waved goodbye as he drove away.

Oh dear. Drug dealers? His girl? A kiss? What had I just gotten myself into?

A Note from Caroline

Thank you so much for taking the time to read this book. I enjoyed writing it and hope that you enjoyed reading it enough to pick up the next in my Miss Prim and Proper Series, A Bayou Wedding.
Thanks to Jana DeLeon for her generosity in sharing her Miss Fortune world with other writers!
To learn more about my other books, please visit my website -
www.carolinemickelson.com[1]
I'd love to have you join my VIP Reader Newsletter so that you can be the first to hear about new releases, discounts, and contests. Join us!

---

1. http://www.carolinemickelson.com